The Adventures of Comanche John

FIVE STAR

Other Five Star Titles by Dan Cushman:

In Alaska with Shipwreck Kelly (1996)
Valley of a Thousand Smokes (1996)
Blood on the Saddle (1998)
The Pecos Kid (1999)
The Pecos Kid Returns (2000)
No Gold on Boothill (2001)

The Adventures of Comanche John

Western Stories

Dan Cushman

Five Star • Waterville, Maine

Additional copyright information on page 224.

Five Star First Edition Western Series.

Published in 2002 in conjunction with Golden West Literary Agency.

Cover design by Thorndike Press Staff.

Set in 11 pt. Plantin.

Printed in the United States on permanent paper.

Library of Congress Cataloging-in-Publication Data

Cushman, Dan.
The adventures of Comanche John : Western stories / by Dan Cushman.
p. cm.
Contents: Comanche John, dead or alive—War bonnet ambush—Smoke talk—Squaw guns—That varmint, Comanche John.
ISBN 0-7862-3536-5 (hc : alk. paper)
1. Outlaws—Fiction. 2. Western stories. I. Title.
PS3553.U738 A65 2002
813′.54—dc21 2002019947

Contents

Editor's Note

Dan Cushman first featured the character Comanche John, a Montana road agent, in "The Conestoga Pirate" in *Frontier Stories* (Winter, 44). In this adventure as well as in the next to appear, "No Gold on Boothill" in *Action Stories* (Summer, 45), he was called Dutch John. Now those two early stories can be found in *No Gold on Boothill* (Five Star Westerns, 2001). It wasn't until publication of "Comanche John—Dead or Alive!" in *Frontier Stories* (Winter, 46) that the character's name was changed to what it would remain in the numerous adventures that followed in various magazines and in three novels: *Montana, Here I Be* (Macmillan, 1950), *The Ripper from Rawhid*e (Macmillan, 1952), and *The Fastest Gun* (Dell First Edition, 1955). In the present volume and *The Return of Comanche John* (Five Star Westerns, 2003), all of the remaining adventures of Comanche John are gathered together for the first time in book form.

Comanche John—Dead or Alive

I

The black-whiskered man nudged his pinto pony down the rocky main street of Skinner's Point at a wary wolf-trot. On reaching the two-story log structure which was evidently the river town's pride, he pulled up and sat for a while, looking around from beneath the droopy brim of his slouch hat. To a casual observer he might have appeared indolent—a loafer on horseback—but his eyes were quick and shrewd, and his grimy hands rested not far from the butts of his two cap-and-ball pistols.

All was quiet. A couple of freight wagons were loading at the Diamond K warehouse. Farther on, where the Missouri River cut a wide arc around the town, three steamboats lay at rest, decks deserted and boilers cold. The black-whiskered man plastered a fragment of white quartz with a spurt of tobacco juice, and chuckled in a manner that showed he was well satisfied.

"Shore peaceful here in Skinner's Point, Patches . . . and peaceful is the way we want her, ain't it?"

Patches lifted one ear in agreement. The saddle leather creaked as the whiskered man reached for the ground with a scuffed jackboot. He looped a rein to the hitch rack in such a manner that a single jerk would loosen it, then he slouched down the corduroy sidewalk. At the door of the stage office, he drew up to squint at a poster.

The poster was large, with big print, and it bore the woodcut likeness of a man. He viewed it from several angles, and took time to gnaw a fresh cheek full from his plug of blackstrap tobacco. By that time a young fellow wearing a leather eyeshade had approached and was about to pass by.

The black-whiskered one hailed him. "Young man, would you mind readin' this here poster? My eddication wasn't such as to include the three Rs."

The young man complied. "It says . . . 'Wanted'. That's the big print across the top. Then beneath the picture it says . . . 'A liberal reward in Yankee Bar dust will be paid for the capture, dead or alive, of one Comanche John, road agent'."

"*One* Comanche John, did you say? Great Jehosaphat, son, is there more'n one of 'em?"

The young man laughed. "No. That's just a formality of speech."

"So that's a picture of Comanche John, is it? He's become some famous of late. Seems like I heerd a song they made up about him." He looked at the face on the poster and chewed disapprovingly. "If they's one thing I can't abide, it's a road agent."

A couple more men had drifted up by this time. They stopped to look at the poster, too. Then a long, loose-jawed fellow came up, wearing a sheriff's star, and the others treated him with deference.

"Admiring him?" the sheriff asked.

"Wouldn't say that," drawled the whiskered one, "but I'd admire some o' that Yankee Bar dust they're givin' in reward. Might pay a man to keep his eye out, if there was enough of it."

The sheriff swaggered a little. "I'd advise this here

Comanche John to stay clear of Skinner's Point, if he wants to stay healthy. Road agents don't last long around here since I got elected."

The whiskered man rolled his chew of blackstrap around in his cheek and squinted at the poster from a couple of new angles. "Unpleasant lookin' varmint, ain't he?"

The sheriff snickered from the side of his big, loose mouth. "Stranger, I was just thinkin' that he looked considerable like you. Now, hold on. No insult intended. But you got to admit there's a considerable similarity."

The black-whiskered man moved around to catch his own reflection in a nearby window. "Waal, now! Maybe you're right. Yes, sir, maybe you are! Why, dingblast their hide . . . what do they mean puttin' my face on that poster? If there was some courts worth the name here in Montana Territory, I'd sue them highbinders over in Yankee Bar. The idee o' puttin' my likeness up thar over the name of a lawless, coach-robbin' reptile like Comanche John. . . ."

"Now, calm down. It ain't the fault of the vigilance committee over at Yankee Bar if you happen to look alike. You wouldn't have a legal leg to stand on."

"I wouldn't? Waal, now, that's a fine state of affairs. What's a gov'ment for? A man has to pay taxes, and then what? . . . he's treated like a criminal!"

"No, sir, not a legal leg. It's nothin' to raise a ruckus about."

"It's all right for you to talk, Sheriff. They ain't got your pitcher up thar bein' slandered by every passerby. A reputation bein' ruint. . . ."

The black-whiskered one was so busy fulminating that he failed to notice the old man who came jogging along on the back of a sleepy mule. He was gaunt and tall with ragged gray whiskers and a pair of piercing, Old Testament eyes. He wore a long black coat, such as gamblers favor—but he was no gambler. His true profession was indicated by the Bible that was thrust in his coat tail pocket.

The talk by the stage office was too ordinary an occurrence to attract his attention, so the preacher continued on down the bumpy street, his head nodding with each step of the mule, his troubled gaze fixed on the distant blue line of bluffs that rose beyond the Missouri. Finally the blaring voice of the black-whiskered man intruded his reverie. He jerked stiffly erect.

"Waal, bless me!" he croaked, reining in and whacking his bony thigh. "It's Comanche John! Why, I heerd they'd hung you over at Last Chance. Glad to see you!"

It was a second before the words registered on the sheriff, but Comanche John did not hesitate. He was on his way down the sidewalk with a series of jack rabbit leaps. He vaulted the hitch rack and loosed the reins while one foot was reaching for the stirrup. The pinto, recognizing an emergency, was away with a snort and a gallop before the seat of John's pants touched the saddle.

"Halt!" bellowed the sheriff, simultaneously going for his right-hand pistol. But a corresponding movement of Comanche John's was swifter. A hitch of his shoulder, that was all, and a Navy was in his hand. He turned in the saddle; a heavy report rocked the afternoon air. The sheriff's gun spun from his hand. He cursed and grabbed his forearm where the lead splinters had burned it. It was three or four seconds before he went for his other gun, and by that time Comanche John was fifty yards away. The sheriff tried to draw a bead. He fired.

At the same instant the pinto stumbled and pawed frantically for a footing. It seemed for a moment that the sheriff's bullet had taken effect, but three rapid puffs of dust far down toward the steamboat docks indicated that it had gone wide —the pinto had been thrown off balance by stepping into a rut. The animal went nose down. For a second he was four hoofs in the air. Comanche John was sent skidding to collide with a hitch post. He was stunned—groggy, but not unconscious. He sat up and fumbled to pull his battered hat away from his face. When he finally got his bearings, the sheriff's Navy was leveled on his heart.

"You're under arrest," panted the sheriff.

Comanche John gathered himself up painfully from the hard roadway. "Yep, Sheriff," he grinned, "it looks like you went and made a hero out of yourself."

The sheriff preened himself for the benefit of the crowd that had been brought out by the excitement. "Told you what would happen if that Comanche John varmint ever showed up at Skinner's Point, didn't I? They may sing songs about him, but he ain't takin' this camp over, by grab! Not while I'm sheriff. Here . . . keep your forepaws away from them guns. I'll take 'em so you won't be tempted. No, Hank, you take 'em while I keep him covered. Thar, that's better. Now I guess I'd better march you down to our new jail before you get any ideas. . . ."

The sky pilot rode up, having urged his mule to a bumpy trot. He hopped off like an animated scarecrow and peered at Comanche John who was caressing a bruised knee with one hand and a skinned shoulder with the other.

"*Humph!* You seem to be in one piece," said the sky pilot.

"One piece! Sure I am, but through no fault o' yourn, you Bible-shoutin' old buzzard. Why couldn't you keep your fly trap shut for a second? I had this big Pike's Peaker of a sheriff eatin' hay out of my pocket. Well, let it go . . . I don't cultivate grudges, but if you choke some night sayin' 'Jeremiah,' don't expect some tears from me."

The old man seemed genuinely sorry. "Don't tell me you're in trouble in this camp, too!"

"Seems I am," moaned John, looking sadly at a rent in his homespuns. "The same old persecution! Now it's that side-windin' gang o' claim jumpers over in Yankee Bar that goes by the name of a vigilance committee. They went and printed up a batch o' posters slanderin' my good name, and sayin' I'd robbed the Last Chance coach. Sheriff, the parson here is familiar with my moral rectitude. Ask him about me. He'll say I'm innocent as a babe unborn. Share and share alike, that's my motto. . . ."

"You can present that plea to the court," the sheriff said smugly. "Judge Doolin will give you plenty chance to talk before he sentences you to hang."

"Sounds like the law here in Skinner's Point has the habit of bein' abrupt," opined Comanche John.

"Our sheriff is sometimes carried away by his enthusiasm!"

This was a new voice—restrained, yet it had a crisp tone that made everyone listen. John watched while a man came toward him, passing with graceful stride through the way the crowd had opened for him. He was tall, handsome, and faultlessly dressed—perhaps no more than thirty-five years old, although his wavy dark hair was already edged with gray. He looked down on John, who was a head shorter, and smiled.

"Contrary to any impression Sheriff Kurdy has given you, the town of Skinner's Point does not execute men without evidence." The tall man turned abruptly on the sheriff who now seemed considerably shrunken in stature. "Kurdy, just what charge do you have against this man?"

When the sheriff hesitated, Comanche John spoke up in a tone of aggrieved dignity: "No evidence whatever. Not a stitch. I came ridin' into this yere camp o' yourn, peaceful as a white-tailed bunny at a rattlesnake's convention, when all of a sudden this hoss-faced varmint with the badge on his jerkin commenced tossin' pistol balls my way. Well, nachilly, me bein' a peaceful man, I. . . . "

Sheriff Kurdy now found his voice: "Do you know who this varmint is, Captain Cutter?"

"I neither know nor care," the captain responded coldly.

This took the sheriff down several notches more. "Why, that's Comanche John . . . Comanche John, the road agent. They'd 'a' hung him in California if he'd stayed, so he shinned out for the Fraser, and, when it got too warm for him there, he. . . ."

John haw-hawed derisively: "Listen to him, Cap'n! Listen to the sheriff thar talk about Californy! Why, he don't even know how to pronounce the name!"

Captain Cutter smiled in his habitually cold manner, and went on to the sheriff: "Well, what if he is Comanche John? What of it?"

"There's a Reward notice posted for him over at the stage office, that's what. He's wanted by the vigilance committee over at Yankee Bar. He robbed the Last Chance coach and. . . ."

Captain Cutter turned abruptly to Comanche John: "Did you rob the Last Chance coach?"

"Me?" Comanche John looked aghast. "So help me, Cap'n, I'm as innocent as a newborn babe!"

The parson made himself heard by snorting several times through his pinched old nostrils, but he managed to hold his tongue. Captain Cutter, however, seemed willing to accept Comanche John's statement. He moved a finely formed hand in a gesture that seemed to say: *Well, that settles that*. He said: "Sheriff, all you actually have against this man is a print shop dodger from Yankee Bar. Yankee Bar happens to be a good distance off, and, anyway, I don't see why we should be running down their suspects for them."

The sheriff shrugged and strode off, muttering. However, some of the onlookers seemed not to give in so easily. Sensing their objections, Cutter turned on them: "Maybe some of you gentlemen think otherwise. If you do, speak up. However, as head of the vigilance committee here, I hold to this principle . . . any man who comes to Skinner's Point is as good as any other. His past is his own business. What's that song I've heard you men singing?" He sang a few lines of the popular frontier ditty, his voice a melodious baritone.

Oh, what was your name in the States?
Was it Thompson, or Johnson, or Yates?
Did you strangle your wife
And run for your life?
Oh, what was your name in the States?

The captain's reasoning produced a wave of disapproval. Several of the men looked nonplused, and several others laughed. It was true—there were many things, besides gold and fur, that sent men West in the 1860s. The captain went on: "If this man behaves himself, I don't care whether he's Comanche John, or Judas. But if he doesn't behave, then I say the sooner he does his polka on the end of a rope, the better."

"Amen," said Comanche John piously. "I hold that a right Christian attitude."

John was given back his guns. The crowd broke up and straggled away. Captain Cutter and the parson watched them go, while Comanche John gravely inspected Patches' fetlocks. Then the captain said to him: "Come to my office in half an hour. It's over the Diamond K warehouse."

Without waiting for an answer, Captain Cutter spun on

the toe of his exquisite boot and strode away along the corduroy sidewalk. In a minute or two, Comanche John and the parson were alone.

"Parson, you'll be the hangin' of me yet," growled John. "By the way, that was a noble gent, that Cap'n. . . ."

"Call him noble, if you like, but I got better words for that varmint."

Comanche John chuckled. "You always did talk thataway about them as didn't come down to the mourner's bench at your mission."

The parson snorted. "That side-wheeler's up to somethin', and, if you want my opinion. . . ."

"Now, Parson,"—John chewed placidly—"don't be too hard on the cap'n. Likely he jest wants to talk over the War for the Confederacy, or such. You know how it is when a couple of Southern gentlemen like he and myself get together."

"He's up to some dirty work, and him wantin' to talk with a road agent like you only proves it."

"Now, Parson. . . ."

"He's crooked as a bull snake, and I don't like his way of doin' business. Take that freight road of his'n which he run up the bluffs yonder. Built it for his Diamond K line, and now he charges the other lines toll so high it puts 'em out of business."

"That's his privilege. He built the road."

"It ain't his privilege to send out that gang of buzzards he calls a vigilance committee to shoot up the Sullivan crew when they tried to build a road of their own."

Comanche John chewed this over silently for a while. He started to say something, but the parson cut him off. "And that's not all. It's only a little part of what he's aimin' to do. Cutter runs this camp of Skinner's Point, as you've already seen. And he also rules the freight road from here to the gold camps. But that ain't enough for a vulture like him. No, sir

. . . now he's aimin' to rule the Missouri clear from here to Saint Louis."

"I've heerd some o' his Diamond K boats," John admitted. "But don't hold it too hard on the cap'n if he should get a bit rough on his competition. It's been a habit with them boat outfits from time to time. I recall once, two or three years back. . . ."

"Competition is fine. I think it's a healthy thing. But not when they start shootin' rival owners in the back, and then turnin' around to rob the same man's pore, innocent daughter of all she's got in the world."

This last was too much for Comanche John. He sank the run-over heels of his jackboots into the dust, and gave a violent hitch to his drooping gun belts. "Rob an innocent gal, did you say? Parson, is that gospel, or are you feedin' me the lump sugar?"

"It's the gospel." The parson then explained in detail. There were three steamboat lines operating between Skinner's Point and St. Louis—the Diamond K, belonging to Captain Cutter; the Arrowhead, owned by young Ross MacLain; and, largest of the three, the Vallon, founded by Pierre Vallon. It was Pierre Vallon who had been murdered near the Arrowhead dock three weeks before. His daughter Lynne was now in charge.

"And you figger Cap'n Cutter is behind his killin'?" asked John.

"I do."

"Ain't sure I can hold with that opinion. What good would it do Cap'n Cutter to shoot this Vallon? It wouldn't put his line out o' business. That gal o' Vallon's inherits the spread, don't she? No, Parson, I think you're sufferin' from a case o' gallopin' delusions. So far, the Cap'n has been a friend o' mine."

The parson snorted. "Then you trust him?"

"I didn't exactly say that." There was a squeak of saddle leather as Comanche John mounted his pony. "Nope . . . he sort o' saved my neck from bein' rope-stretched, so that makes him a friend o' the first water, but I ain't in the habit o' trustin' my friends."

"If you can't trust your friends, who do you trust?" grumbled the parson. "Nobody?"

"Me? Sure I trust somebody. I trust my enemies." Comanche John let the parson stew over this for a while, then he beat his thigh and roared out a coarse laugh. The pinto started drifting along the street. "Whar's your church located, Parson?" John called over his shoulder.

"T'other side of the Sandbar Saloon."

"Mebby I'll drop in after a bit. We can drink whisky and sing a psalm together."

II

Comanche John selected a cigar from a box of Cuban perfectos and sniffed it like a connoisseur. Cutter held out his candle cigar lighter, but John shook his head. He spat out his chew of blackstrap, ground the cigar to a leafy pulp between his palms, and selected a generous cheek full. The remainder he dumped into the pocket of his homespuns. "If they's one thing I enjoy more'n another," he remarked, "it's a fine cee-gar."

"So I see." Cutter smiled. He lit his own cigar, and puffed for a while. "So you're Comanche John," he mused, settling back and tapping the floor with one boot toe.

"Yep, the gen-u-wine."

"I've been hearing about you for some time."

"I ain't surprised." John chewed. "They even made up a

song about me. It's powerful pretty. Goes like this." He commenced to sing in a wavering, wolf-like falsetto.

Comanche John was born
In the state of Tennessee,
The son of humble mountain folk
Who lived in pover-tee;
Young John hit out for Kansas
At the age of twenty-three
To vote in the election
On the side of slaver-ee.
He wandered to Texas
With a pal named Injun Ike. . . .

Cutter broke in and said: "I've already heard the ballad, I believe."

"Chances are you ain't heered the verse about when I robbed the coach at Pistol Rock. It was made up by a muleskinner over at Montana City. It goes. . . ."

"Never mind." Cutter looked at John thoughtfully for a while. "You're fully aware that I saved you from hanging out there a few minutes ago."

"Yep! And I'm downright grateful."

"I don't doubt you deserved to hang."

"Thank-ee."

"By reputation you're a pretty fancy man with your Navies."

"Waal . . . I've shot at bottles, here and there."

"I have a proposition for a man like you. I want you to lead a certain group for an evening . . . negligible risk, substantial consideration."

"Would you mind dealin' that hand over? Them big cyards flew by so fast I couldn't read the spots on 'em."

Cutter smiled. "All right . . . how'd you like an easy job for the heavy color?"

"Now, that's my language. Just what was you figgerin' to rob, Cap'n, a faro bank, a stagecoach, or a steamboat?"

"Rob?" Cutter nodded. "Well, perhaps a person would call it robbery. If so, it's a steamboat."

Comanche John rubbed his palms jubilantly. "I've always hankered to rob me a steamboat. Think what a verse that would make for my song!"

"And we're going to sink the boat, too."

"Sink it! Is that really necessary?"

Cutter did not answer. He strode to a closet and lifted the lid of a trunk. It was filled with clothing popular with sailors and officers on river steamboats. He tossed John a pair of dungaree trousers, a blue shirt, and a stiff-billed cap. Comanche John noticed that the cap was marked by an Arrowhead insignia.

"Thought your line was the Diamond K."

"It is. And that cap is an Arrowhead. That's why you will wear it tomorrow night . . . when you direct the sinking of that Vallon boat."

"I'm beginnin' to catch on," John said, chewing slowly. He splattered Cutter's spotless floor with tobacco juice, and chewed some more. "Yep, I'm mighty quick in the head when it comes to thinkin'. Our boys dress up like Arrowhead men, we sink the Vallon boat, and then you sit back and let your two competitors battle right down to their last bottom. Why, that's smart! You'll be in position to rule the river from. . . ."

Cutter broke in: "You can leave the long-range plans to me. Your job is to put that boat to the bottom. If you do, you'll be paid a thousand dollars. The boat you're to sink is Vallon's *White Cloud*. She'll take on some furs and then cross to Coalmine Point for buffalo hides. I expect her to get away from there about sundown. Anyway, you'll have plenty of time to cross the Horseshoe Bend and attack her when she runs close to the shore at the mouth of Assiniboine Coulée."

"Undoubtless I get a cut on the furs we take off her."

"You'll get your thousand dollars," Cutter snapped.

"Sorry I brung the matter up." John chewed, his voice resigned, but his eyes as cold as a winter's sky. "By the way, Cap'n, ain't this Vallon line owned by a gal? A Miss Lynne Vallon, daughter of old Pierre? And didn't I hear she was castin' sheep's eyes at Ross MacLain, owner of Arrowhead?"

Cutter made an impatient gesture. "May I remind you of something? Yankee Bar would still like very much to get its hands on you. I saved you from a rope this afternoon. I might not be quite so solicitous if anything went wrong. Do we understand each other?"

"Cap'n, we heap savvy each other from the head box right down across the riffles."

"Good!" Cutter stood with a gesture that indicated the meeting was finished. "There'll be about fifteen men to help you. We should have more, but men you can trust are sometimes hard to find. I want you to get together with them tonight in the cabin of the warehouse. Be there at twelve o'clock or a little after."

Ten minutes later Comanche John clomped his dusty jackboots the length of the parson's mission and sat heavily in the front pew. "Parson," he stated, "I've always been proud of my strength of stomach, but I'm bound to admit that Cap'n Cutter is too much for my de-gestion."

The parson made an "I-told-you-so" sound in his throat, and then listened while John outlined Cutter's plan.

"What do you aim to do about it?" he asked when John had finished.

"I ain't exactly decided. I'm tore this way and that. You see, I'm indebted to Cutter for savin' my life . . . and a debt's a debt, as the Injuns say. If it hadn't been for that, I'd lean toward shootin' him. Though there's this way of lookin' at it, too . . . if I don't shoot him, that means I'm savin' his life, sort of, so it makes us even all over again."

"There'll be no bloodshed if I can help it," snapped the parson. "It's always the same thing whenever I run into you. It was that way at Lemhi, and it was that way at Eldorado."

"And it'll end by bein' that way here at Skinner's Point. It's the only way ag'in' varmints like Cutter."

"Them which lives by the sword shall die by the sword," insisted the parson.

"They's somethin' else the Good Book says, Parson. An eye tooth for an eye tooth, that's what."

"Just the same, I got me an idee. A man don't necessarily need guns if he uses his head."

John lolled back in the log pew and freshened the chew of tobacco in his cheek. "Waal, don't feel hurt if I sort of keep my Navies handy just in case."

That evening Comanche John insisted on visiting the jail. "Never yet seen a skookum house that could hold me," he explained to Sheriff Kurdy, "so I sort of drop around and have a look whenever I get in a new camp."

The sheriff hee-hawed and whacked his leg. "Never seen a jail that could hold him, he says. Waal, you're lookin' at one right now. See them walls? . . . eighteen inches thick. And the bars! . . . they was hammered from steel left over when the *Memphis Gal* busted her boilers. I reckon maybe you're a foxy customer like the song about you says, but you couldn't bust this jail between now and doomsday. . . . Hey! What you doin' there?"

John lowered the loose plank he had lifted from the floor. "Just inspectin'. And about me bustin' this jail betwixt now and doomsday . . . I look upon that as a personal challenge."

"You do?"

"Yep. I aim to personally crack this prison before I leave the fine, upstandin' city of Skinner's Point."

When they were outside, the parson complained: "That was the most foolish brag I ever heard. And what the thunder does any man want to go around inspectin' jails for?"

"P'fessional interest, Parson. I'm interested in jails just like you're interested in churches . . . I'm in and out of 'em so much. Now, about this Ross MacLain. You say he owns the Arrowhead line. You suppose we ought to drop around and visit that young bucko . . . after dark, of course?"

Ross MacLain, owner of the Arrowhead steamboat line, was not usually a nervous young man, but tonight he was on edge. He'd been on edge frequently of late—ever since Pierre Vallon had been murdered. Strange thing, that murder of Vallon, shot in the back, and not for money, either, for there was gold in his pockets when they found him, and Vallon wasn't a man with many enemies. Ross felt sorry for Pierre's daughter—Lynne—all alone in the world, running a steamboat line from a tough frontier camp like Skinner's Point. Ross had been so sympathetic that he'd called on her every evening that week—each time staying a little later. This night he stayed so long that Mama Annie, Lynne's old nurse and self-appointed protector, had cast certain hints. It was eleven-thirty, Annie had pointed out, and a young man who stayed at a girl's home until such an hour certainly cared little for her reputation. So Ross waited until Annie had stalked from the room, resisted an impulse to kiss the owner of the Vallon Line, pressed her hand instead, and started for the docks.

The *White Cloud* was tied up at the Vallon dock. Her boilers were being fired, preparatory to leaving next morning. A couple hundred yards farther along at his own dock lay the *Highland Mary*, a dark hulk no longer fit for the bars and cross-currents of the "Wild Mizzouree." Ross had fixed up a suite of cabins in her and lived there in considerable luxury.

He climbed the short plank to her deck. A shadow emerged and moved toward him. "Jocko?"

"So, *M'zhu* Ross."

Jocko was a gargantuan French-Indian-mulatto whom Ross had rescued from the ship of a Caribbean slave smuggler south of New Orleans three years before. As this was the only kindness he had ever received, Jocko had since followed him with the devotion of a spaniel.

Ross walked to his quarters with Jocko half a step in the lead. There the big mulatto opened the door and stood at attention as he had seen soldiers do. The stateroom Ross entered was furnished as befitted the bachelor owner of a half-million-dollar steamboat line. He bid Jocko good night, closed the door, and stretched out in his favorite armchair. He smoked a pipe and went to bed.

It seemed he had been asleep scarcely a minute when he was aroused by the sound of Jocko's voice, crying out in a wild mixture of English, French, and heaven only knew what. Then another voice, bellowing whole mouthfuls of oaths.

Ross located his pistol and ran on deck. He drew up in surprise on seeing the huge Jocko on hands and knees, rising groggily from the floor. Standing back a few steps and partly hidden in the shadows was a heavy-booted fellow with tangled black whiskers.

"Thar's a lesson I learnt from the Arapahoes," the black-whiskered one was saying. "Look for it next time you come for somebody with a knife."

Ross advanced quietly on bare feet. "Drop your gun, stranger," he commanded.

"Which one?" There was a laugh in the bewhiskered man's voice. "The one I got on you, or the one I got on your man, yonder?"

It was true. The whiskered one was holding a Navy pistol in each hand. Then, to make his situation more precarious, another man moved in the shadow right by his elbow.

"Don't jump like that, MacLain," chuckled black whiskers, "the parson, yonder, is right peaceful."

A gray man with a thin, beaked face now stepped into the moonlight.

"Why, it's the missionary from over town!" Ross exclaimed.

"The same!" answered the parson. "And yonder fellow is a more or less heathenish friend o' mine. I mostly endure his nee-ferious habits and put some of 'em to the cause of Christian betterment. His handle is Comanche John."

"Seems like I've heard of you. . . ."

"Yep, it's likely you have." John spat across the deck for emphasis. "They even made up a hymn about me. Every muleskinner and bullwhacker betwixt here and Salt Lake is singin' it. Right pretty. Goes like this."

Comanche John rode to I-dee-ho
In the year of 'Sixty-Two
With a pal named Whisky Anderson
And one called Jake-the. . . .

"Never mind," yowled the parson. "We got more important things than that song. Where's your sleepin' room, MacLain?"

Ross took them inside and listened while John told of his meeting with Captain Cutter. He was grim when the story was finished.

"The *White Cloud* leaves tomorrow about daylight. I think they plan on stopping at Coalmine Point to take on buffalo hides. I don't imagine they'll get away from there before sundown. They'll take it easy through the night because the pilot will want to run the narrows by daylight. I guess that would put them opposite Assiniboine Coulée about midnight." He stood up. "I'd better warn Lynne tonight."

John snorted. "And let Cutter and his gang slip away? We got to catch 'em with the evidence or Cutter will cook up some new deviltry. Say nothin' to the gal, that's my counsel. Let Cutter go ahead and get his neck in the noose. All we need do is round up twelve or fifteen men we can trust and hide 'em in the brush back of Assiniboine Coulée. When Cutter and his boys are busy, waltz in on 'em."

"Ought to be easy as 'rithmetic to a schoolmarm," agreed the parson.

Ross thought it over for a while and agreed. They worked out a few details of the plan, then he called: "Paytee!"

"And who, pray, is Paytee?" asked John.

"A Polynesian boy who cooks for me."

Paytee was short, sleek, and obsequious, although not so young as the word "boy" would indicate. He glided in after only a few seconds' wait.

"You dress in a hurry!" said Ross.

"I hear big fight. Then I know you have company. So. . . ."

"Fine! Stir up some coffee. And bring us a bottle of that sherry I got in Saint Louis."

Comanche John and the parson stayed for half an hour.

Ross followed them to the plank, and a few minutes later he left, also. He wanted to look up some trusted men for the next evening's business. The boat was quiet. Perhaps an hour passed—then there came a soft, gurgling sound like something being lowered in the water. Jocko, who kept watch, made no move to investigate. Such sounds were common in moving water at night. He had no reason to suspect that the soft gurgle had come from the gentle descent of the Polynesian, Paytee, sliding from the far side of the boat.

Paytee stroked easily, in a frog-fashion, without lifting hands or feet from the water. He let the current sweep him downstream for a hundred yards, then he turned sharply and struck out for shore with a swift crawl stroke. Once ashore he slid quickly into the shadow of a cottonwood grove and followed a roundabout route that took him to the stairway of Captain Cutter's apartment in the town.

Paytee didn't stay long in the apartment. In five minutes he sneaked back down the stairs and ran to the river upstream from the boat. Jocko was still standing near the plank when he floated down and pulled himself up the side. The entire trip had not consumed twenty-five minutes.

Back in his apartment, Captain Cutter sat on the edge of his bed, his handsome face more than usually grim. He bit an end from one of his long cigars with a grimace that indicated his vexation. He puffed thoughtfully, and the frown was replaced by a gloating smile. He snapped his fingers in a gesture that indicated he knew quite well what his course would be.

III

The steamboat *White Cloud* got underway about mid-morning and headed across the river to Coalmine Point for its buffalo hides. She lay there all afternoon, her tall chimneys trailing a haze of smoke. Toward evening the haze thickened and the chimneys rolled billowing black. The *White Cloud* put on steam, and nosed her way into the current.

"About time for me to heave-ho," remarked John to the parson. "I got to get Cap'n Cutter's boys together if we're to cut across the horseshoe bend in time to catch that craft at Assiniboine. But first off, I think I'll get me some eatin' tobacco."

John and the parson stepped from the store to ram against twin guns held in the hands of Sheriff Kurdy.

"Skinner's Point must be a rough camp," John drawled innocently. "Imagine a sheriff havin' to carry his pistols on the ends of his arms instead of in his holsters."

"You're under arrest."

"Me!" John seemed scandalized. He edged over toward the door of a harness shop. "Reckon I must have mistook what you. . . ."

"Stand back from thar!" roared Kurdy. "Don't get the idea I wouldn't just hanker pullin' these triggers?"

Two deputies appeared from hiding places behind the store. They, like the sheriff, were taking no chances. Their guns were drawn. One of them lifted John's two Navies.

"Better look under his coat," Kurdy said. "He had a hide-out Derringer there yesterday."

"None there today." The deputy turned his attention to the parson. "And this old pelican don't carry armaments at all. Only thing he's armed with is Scripture."

"This is an outrage!" squawked the parson.

"I'll say it's an outrage!" John roared in agreement. "Me, one of the most outstandin' and famous men in the whole Nor'west. . . ."

"Mebby," said Kurdy with a smug smile, "but in an hour or two you will be *was* famous, if you understand what I'm drivin' at."

"And what crime have I done?"

"Just because you ain't committed a crime yet don't mean you can't be hung. You intended to, and intention is accessory after the act, as it says in the revised statutes."

John chewed and squinted at the sheriff. "It also says in them stat-choots o' yourn that a prisoner, when accosted by an officer of the law, must be informed by said officer, to wit . . . the charge and reason for said incarceration. Ain't that Hoyle, Parson?"

"Right!" the parson cackled.

"We don't go that far into Hoyle or Blackstone or them old side-wheelers here in Skinner's Point. But you'll be hung legal. Judge Doolin will see to that." Kurdy bowed with mock solemnity. "Would you please inspect our jail, Mister Comanche John? Seems like I overheard a brag you made about it not bein' able to hold you."

The jail was a good one. The bars were strap metal, bolted to thick, cottonwood logs. The door was heavy, whipsawed plank reinforced with strips of steel, and it was secured on the outside by a solid beam and a padlock.

Kurdy snapped that padlock and looked inside at John and the parson with a satisfied smirk. "Still think you can bust her?"

"Guess I talked out of tune," John admitted contritely.

Kurdy chortled for a while, and then left to brag about his

arrest at some of the barrooms.

"Why'd you tell him you could break this jail?" asked the parson. "A fat chance we got now. He's got a double guard posted."

"Don't rile me, Parson. If it weren't for your pious plan to run a crusade down the main street of this mangy river town, I wouldn't even be in this jail. I'd be out, earnin' an honorable livin' robbin' stagecoaches."

The parson waved a knuckly old finger under John's nose. "You'll come to no good end, breakin' the laws of the land and braggin' about it."

John hee-hawed and beat dust from the leg of his homespun pants. "Parson, I hate to remind you, but if I don't fulfill my brag and get us out of this cage, we'll both come to that 'no good end' you mentioned. Yep, we'll both do our final quadrille at the end of a rope."

The gray part of evening was settling in. One of the deputies lit a candle in the jail office. Its yellow flame cast a few weak rays through the barred opening in the cell door. The parson sat on the edge of a bunk, head in hands, thinking. For a space of fifteen minutes, neither he nor Comanche John spoke. Out in the office a *slap-slap* of cards indicated that the deputy was playing solitaire. A freight wagon creaked past, and the muleskinner sang in a sad voice. The words made John sit up very straight.

"Glory be, Parson," he chortled, "d'ye hear the hymn that 'skinner is singin'?"

The muleskinner's voice became louder as his wagon creaked along the rutted street.

Comanche John came to I-dee-ho
In the year of 'Sixty-Two

With a pal named Whisky Anderson
And one called Jake-the-Shoe.
Three straighter shootin' highwaymen
The Nor'west never knew
Oh, listen to my stor-e-e-e
I'll tell ye what they do.
They rode to Orofino
On the old Snake River trail,
They robbed the coach at Pistol Rock
And stopped the western mail,
But Jake got drunk in Lewiston
And ended up in jail,
And they hung him to a cottonwood
'Fore John could go his bail.

The muleskinner stopped singing and commenced hurling imprecations at his beasts, and the parson remarked: "A fitting conclusion."

"Imagine, tryin' to hold me in jail," John muttered. "*Me,* the hero of every muleskinner from Salt Lake to Bignose."

The minutes stretched out. There seemed to be an unusual amount of activity out in the street. "Maybe they're riggin' up to hang us," remarked John, trying to see the street from the tiny window. "What's going on in this camp, anyhow?" he asked the guard.

"Posse," came back the reply.

"Who for?"

"For your pards. For the men who hired you to come here."

"Hired me! Deal that one over."

"Don't act innocent. Cap'n Cutter found out the plans that you and your preacher pal made with Ross McLain to rob and sink that Vallon steamboat up by Medicine Grove, and. . . ."

"By Medicine Grove!" the parson cackled.

"Sit down, Parson. Ain't you never heard it's impolite to interrupt folks?" John apologized to the guard. "Don't pay heed to my pard, here. You know how these old Bible-totin' buzzards be. Always thinks he's at camp meetin'. Next thing, he'll get the shakes. What was it you was about to say? I'm sort of anxious to find out how much of our plans he had figured."

"Might as well," said the guard, tossing down his deck. "You'll be hung in another hour, anyhow."

"Sure," John agreed. "We'll be lifeless as salt mackerel. Now where did you say this steamboat sinkin' was to take place?"

"Medicine Grove. Cap'n Cutter was certain you and your men would be waitin' for her there. After the job was done, you planned to scatter and meet up again at Assiniboine."

"Say, ain't he the smart one!"

"None smarter! But wait till you hear what he aims to do. First, the vigilance riders head off the boat. Then he sends a posse to surround Assiniboine. So you see, he has your bunch, MacLain and all. Has 'em both ways. If he's too late to head 'em off at Medicine Grove, he'll round 'em up at Assiniboine!"

"Whipsawed! Why, that's purty. D'ye hear that, Parson? D'ye hear how smart the cap'n is?"

"Medicine Grove," muttered the Parson.

John whispered: "Sure, the cap'n will sink her there hisself, then he'll ride on and nab Ross and his boys at Assiniboine like sittin' ducks. It's slick as beaver mud."

"What'll we do?" wailed the parson.

John did not answer. He slouched there by the cell door, chewing, but his eyes, when the candlelight struck them, were shrewd and calculating.

The posse was still gathered in the street. There were impatient movements of hoofs, repressed excitement in the voices of the men. Soon they galloped away. The town seemed deserted for a while, then the *squeak* of fiddles and the *twang* of banjos made themselves heard from the nearby hurdy-gurdy houses; men sang and talked and walked the sidewalks—Skinner's Point had returned to normal.

By the *slap-slap* of cards in the office they knew that the guard still played solitaire. The other guard loitered near the wall outside.

"Don't worry," said Comanche John to the parson. "A Gypsy gal in Frisco told my fortune one time and said I was goin' to die in bed . . . betwixt them white things quality folks sleeps in."

"Sheets?"

"Yep. And with a goose-hair pillow beneath my head!"

"T'ain't bein' hung which worries me," the parson moaned. "I keep thinkin' about poor Ross McLain and that Vallon gal. Them dependin' on us, and us in jail."

John stood and walked tiptoe to peer from the window. The guard still lurked around outside. John cursed and paced the cell.

"Reckon I'll have to chance it," he muttered.

"Chance what?"

"Not so loud, you idjit! You ain't preachin' a sermon."

"Chance what?" the parson whispered.

"Chance escapin'."

The parson hopped up on his spindly old legs. "You got some way of gettin' out of here?"

John shuffled across the floor, seeming to feel for something with his heavy, horsehide jackboots. One plank appeared to interest him, for, after squeaking up and down on it a few times, he bent over, lifted it, and felt beneath. It was the same plank he had lifted when inspecting the jail the day before. When he stood, a stray beam of light reflected from the blued barrel of a big-bore Texas Derringer.

"Well, glory be," gasped the parson.

IV

Comanche John swaggered around the cell a few times. "Yep! This ought to be a lesson to you, Parson. You should never question my actions. I had me a reason for inspectin' this here cage last night. It's my regular policy to slip a gun inside the jail whenever I visit a doubtful camp. Shucks, I got me Derringers hid under floors and inside mattresses and betwixt logs of jails from Yuba City to Canady. Cheap little cannons, these, but load 'em with buck and they're mean potent at squaw's range." John chuckled and beat the leg of his homespuns. "Oh, I'm the smart one when it comes to thinkin'."

John suddenly seized the parson, shook him like a bulldog shaking a poodle, and stamped his jackboots while he roared: "Gimme that poke, gol dang ye! Parson, that thar gold is half mine!"

The parson protested and gasped for breath. "Lemme alone," he wailed, perhaps thinking John had gone insane. By that time the guard had thrown down his cards and was trying to see inside. "Hey, cut out that racket. . . ."

"It's gold, and it's half mine," John panted. He turned to the guard for judgment. "He found a poke o' gold under the pallet, yonder. "It's half and half, ain't it, Deppity?"

The second guard shouted from outside: "What's the matter in there, Hank?"

"Nothing!" Hank hastened to answer him. He was itching

to get his hands on the gold. "Stand by yonder wall!" he commanded.

John and the parson obeyed. The deputy then unbolted the door and entered, gun in hand. "Such property becomes confiscated by law. Where is this dust?"

"Loaded in these two bar'ls," John drawled, leveling his double Derringer. "An ounce in each of 'em, and, if you make one wrong move, you'll take possession right betwixt the eyes."

The deputy stood there, jaw drooping. His fingers slowly relaxed, and the gun he was holding *clunked* to the floor.

"Get it, Parson," said John. "And get the one on his hip, too."

"What's a-goin' on in thar, Hank?" demanded the outside deputy, trying to see through the window.

John jiggled his Derringer significantly. "Come on . . . tell the man."

"N-nothing," answered Hank. "Just a little argument I had to settle."

Satisfied, the guard shuffled away. The parson breathed deeply and paused with Hank's second pistol, undecided what he should do with it. He ended by sticking it in the band of his pants.

"Parson,"—John chuckled—"now you look mighty nigh human."

"Let's get ourselves out of here," squawked the parson in his parrot voice.

John clapped his hand over the parson's mouth, but it was too late. The guard had overheard. They could hear him mutter something and start toward the jail door. John waited, a Navy in one hand and the Derringer in the other, but the guard decided not to go in.

After a few seconds, John motioned for the parson to

follow him from the cell. He turned to bolt the door. For a second they were visible from the office window. John sensed a movement outside and flung the parson flat against the wall just as the guard fired. The air was filled with stinging fragments of glass. Almost simultaneously John's Navy roared—but he did not aim at the window. The bullet cut the candle wick.

Everything was flickered into darkness. They waited. Slowly a long rectangle of light emerged to mark the location of the open door, and two smaller rectangles, the windows. Everything seemed quiet. John moved out the front door, and the parson followed him.

By this time, both guards were shouting for help. Attracted by their cries, men ran from several doorways. A big, florid fellow wearing a pearl-gray stovepipe hat was bellowing with the volume of a Fourth-of-July orator and waving his arms. "It's over at the jail. What are you waiting for? It's those two road agents, gentlemen! Over there in a hurry, I say, and check that escape!"

"Lead the way, Judge," chuckled a muleskinner. "Every army needs a general, I reckon, and you're the ranking officer now that lord-high Cap'n Cutter has gone."

Others in the crowd did not share the muleskinner's caution. They ran around the corner of the saloon with guns drawn. The outside guard now made himself heard, his voice coming from behind a rubbish pile midway between the jail and the street. "They're out front somewheres. Fan out a little and don't get too close. That black-whiskered gent is a killer from away back."

"Nonsense!" the judge boomed from a hiding place he had chosen behind a rain barrel. "Why exercise caution at a moment like this? Close in, I say. Close in, men, and take them dead or alive!"

The night was filled with shadowy forms, moving slowly to surround the jail. John, pulling the parson after him, moved along in the shadow of the building until he was only a few steps from the rubbish pile where the guard was hiding.

"Drop yore pistols, Deppity." He grinned.

The deputy, who had thought John was making his escape in the other direction, muttered something and obeyed. John hopped over the rubbish heap, took one of the deputy's pistols for himself, and tossed the other to the parson.

"Thar," he said with evident satisfaction, slapping his weighted holsters, "reckon that balances me up proper again. Come along, Parson."

They edged on tiptoe past some buildings until they were far from the jail, and then hurried downhill to the riverfront. "What's the idee?" the parson panted after they had covered fifty yards or so. "We got to find hosses, ain't we . . . ?"

"Hosses, nothin'! You can't follow the river bluffs on horseback. Nope, I noticed one of them Diamond K boats pullin' up from downriver this evenin', and unless she lost her head o' steam quicker'n I anticipate, you and me, we're goin' to ride down the Mizzouri in style."

It was the *Sioux Scout* just in from St. Louis. She had finished unloading, and all except a couple of her crew had headed up the street toward the town's houses of pleasure. While John and the parson watched, these two left the boat and went through the wide door of a warehouse where a lamp was burning.

John motioned for the parson to follow him aboard the boat. They made a swing around the deck, but it was deserted. "Gimme a hand, Parson. These hawsers are pulled plenty tight."

The parson helped him loosen the hawsers. For a while the

boat drifted slowly. Then her stern swung outward in a gentle arc, the current caught her, and she was swept swiftly toward midstream. It all happened so quickly that no one on the docks noticed what had happened until the *Sioux Scout* had just about disappeared into the darkness.

"Waal, Parson,"—Comanche John grinned—"I don't reckon it's every day a man steals himself a steamboat! That's gettin' way up in the higher reaches o' banditry. Think what a verse this'll make for the song they're singin' about me."

Comanche John stole a riverboat,
A sternwheel Diamond K,
A braver piece o'. . . .

"Hush up! They's somebody below!"

They listened. A man was bellowing down in the engine room. "I tell you they've cut this craft loose! I'm goin' topside and see what's got into their fool heads. Hire a gang o' punkin-rollers for crew, and what do you get?"

He kept cursing and bellowing as his heavy boots *clomped* up the boiler hatch. He stood on the deck and looked around—a soot-encrusted man clad only in boots, pants, and a boatman's cap.

"Who are *you?*" he demanded on seeing John.

"Comanche John's the handle."

John waited for the engineer to be confounded by the announcement, but the man merely looked blank.

"Ain't you never heered o' me? They sure have some ignorant men on this river! Waal, I'll bet gold to greenbacks you'll hear about me after tonight."

"What you doin' on this craft?" the engineer finally got around to bellowing. "Where's the cap'n? Git out of my way, you muleskinner. . . ."

The engineer started to push past, but something about John's attitude caused him to change his mind.

"I'm master o' this craft now," John told him, "and I want some steam. Parson, you git yonder to the pilot house and take the wheel."

John clomped to the boiler room behind the engineer and looked around. "Git some pitch pine in that furnace," he shouted at a surprised Negro lad whose task it was to stoke the boilers. "Go on, git . . . !"

"You can't put in more wood!" objected the engineer.

"Why?"

"Look at the steam gauge. That left boiler ain't so good. Five more pounds and you'll blow her head clean off."

"Don't tell me what I can do. I'm cap'n o' this here steamboat now, and I want some speed out of her. Weight that safety valve. Throw on more wood. Git the paddlewheel to turnin'. We got to catch the *White Cloud* before she gets out o' the bluffs!"

Under the threat of John's pistols, an anvil was hung on the safety valve. The Negro boy heaved in pitch pine. John seated himself on the bottom step of the hatch and chewed placidly.

The *Sioux Scout* was a new boat, designed to battle the Missouri's swift current, and tonight, with that current at her stern, she went booming along at a clip few riverboats could equal. For several miles after leaving Skinner's Point the channel was deep and quite regular. By simply keeping the craft to the middle of the stream, the parson had no difficulty. Then the river made a slow swing to the right toward a spot known to river men as Smoke Creek Crossing. The channel here was constantly shifting. Where it lay deep and safe one week, it might be choked the next. As a result, more timorous pilots were in the habit of sending a skiff ahead to sound passage. The parson, however, slowed not a turn of the paddle-wheel. He swung his churning craft into the crossing with all the daring that could be derived from complete ignorance. So, while any pilot, drunk or sober, knew that the most likely course hugged the south bank, the parson steered down the middle. All the while the engineer waved his arms from the engine room hatch and screamed: "Hug the bank! Hug back to starboard."

"Which side's that?" asked the parson.

But John elbowed the engineer out of his way. "Don't worry your head about our pilot, yonder. He's got Providence on his side, I reckon." Then he roared up to the pilot house: "Let her have both bar'ls, Parson!"

The boat was of shallow draft. In addition, she had just been relieved of her cargo, and hence she rode high in the water. Perhaps this was her salvation, for she skimmed the treacherous bars of the crossing and churned through to the deeper waters beyond.

V

The river followed a sharp cleft between dark clay bluffs. It was here they hoped to overtake the *White Cloud*, but mile after mile slipped away and the river was only a strip of darkness ahead. Gradually the bluffs fell away, and they came to a wild badlands country of barren, pointed hills. The river here was wider, its current diminished, and it kept breaking into separate channels with narrow, cottonwood-covered islands between. The parson mumbled a prayer and steered among them.

"Parson! You aim a steamboat like I aim a pistol ball!" roared John.

But the parson did not answer. His jaw was set, chin whiskers bristling, and his eyes cut the darkness to a spot a couple of miles distant where a string of lights wavered along the water's edge. After a few seconds, John spotted it, too.

"Blast ye, Parson, that's it. They've stopped the *White Cloud* already, but I reckon we'll be there in time to raise a ruckus." He bellowed more orders down to the engineer: "Put on steam! I've seen more hiss in a teakettle. And don't give me none o' yore lip or I'll use ye for pistol practice."

The river was wide—shallow. Even the parson's unpracticed eye could detect the moonlit riffles and streaks of dead water where the shoals lay. Areas of cattails and first-year willows occupied the crests of the larger bars and mud banks. The farther he steered, the more apparent it became that the real channel lay against the south bank. The *White Cloud* was over there, and in order to reach her he would need to do one of two things—either continue downstream until he reached the main channel, or risk crossing the wide shallows.

The parson steered on for a while, praying for some favorable development. He watched hopefully as some of the mud flats dwindled, but, outweighing this favorable sign, a long, narrow island came into view, cutting the river in half. Appearance of the island made the parson realize his moment for decision had come. With an abrupt heave on the wheel he brought the craft around across the current, and in another thirty seconds she was cutting through quiet, shoal water.

There was little to spare. Twice the bottom of the long boat ground against sandbars, but in both cases her momentum carried her over. After what seemed to be a long time, the head of the island crept past, and they slid into the deep water of the south channel.

"Glory be!" marveled John. "Providence is shore with ye tonight. And thar's the *White Cloud*, yonder, hung up on a sandbar just so we can catch her."

The *White Cloud* lay cross-stream and down two hundred yards. The bright light of her furnace doors was visible, and her ports were all aglow. The moonlight glistened from her paddlewheel as it churned fruitlessly against the sandbar. The parson rang bells, and the paddle of the *Sioux Scout* was cut. He shouted down: "John, I believe that's Cutter's men ridin' toward her now."

"Where? I can't see 'em."

"Just splashin' over from the shore."

John clomped to the hurricane deck for a view. Sure enough—there was a gang of men, riding through the shallow water that separated the *White Cloud* from the shore. He chuckled and beat on his pants leg.

"What'll we do?" the parson wailed.

"Do? Why, Parson, this here is pretty. It's beautiful. We couldn't have ast for nothin' better. Wheel cross-stream a bit, gee-haw her around, and lay her betwixt the *White Cloud* and the bank. If our wave don't dislodge that boat, you can call me a Blackfoot and shoot me dead."

"But how about us?"

"What you worryin' about? It ain't *your* boat, is it?"

The parson rang for the paddles and aimed the craft as Comanche John had directed, wheeling her so sharply that one side of the hull ground against the gravel of the river bottom. She loomed unexpectedly to Cutter's men who had been intent on the *White Cloud*. Someone shouted an alarm. They tried to bring their horses around, fighting the current and sand. A couple splashed on toward the *White Cloud*. The others headed for shore. It was a mix-up of men and horses.

"Yip-e-e!" shouted John. "Clear out of the way, you hossback pirates, hyar we come!"

The parson had now straightened the boat out, and she

was running full blast with the rapid current. The captain of the *White Cloud*, still not understanding the madman's scene that had developed, was shouting warnings through his megaphone, but the parson paid no heed. He kept the boat roaring toward the shallow stretch of muddied river that separated the *White Cloud* from shore—water still filled with plunging horses, terrified riders.

The prow of the parson's boat shot past the stern of the *White Cloud*. They came abreast. For a second it seemed that, miraculously, the *Sioux Scout* would skim over the sandbar, but then, with a roar and a splinter of timbers, she plowed herself deeper and came to a shuddering stop.

Comanche John picked himself up from the deck in time to see the great swell of water carry the churning *White Cloud* up with momentary buoyancy. She slid forward half her length on the crest of it, sank again, lower than before, her paddlewheels flinging mud, and then, with a brave effort, freed herself and sped on downstream.

"Come on, Parson! Let's get ourselves out of here before them varmints o' Cutter's decide to put us on as an entertainment!"

The parson half climbed, half fell from the pilot house. "Where's the *White Cloud?*" he asked.

"Gone, Parson." Then John stopped and cursed. The *White Cloud* had eased off a couple hundred yards away and was evidently getting ready to drop anchor.

"Git goin'!" John shouted. When he realized they couldn't hear him, he drew one of his pistols and commenced firing. These bullets must have carried his message, for the boat lost no time getting out of range.

By now the forces of Captain Cutter were rallying near shore. "That's my boat!" Cutter was shouting. "That's the *Sioux Scout*. I heard Comanche John up there. Board that boat, damn you! Don't let those men get away."

Comanche John and the parson leaped from the hurricane deck, intending to escape ashore. The parson threw one leg over the rail, but John stopped him. "We'll have to get aft!"

"Hold on," yipped the Parson. "They're comin' from that end, too."

One of Cutter's vigilantes caught sight of them and cut loose with his pistol. The lead thudded against timbers. Comanche John's right hand pistol roared an answer. The vigilante crumpled, and his plunging horse dragged him away, his foot hanging in the stirrup.

"One!" said John. "How many more we got to go, Parson?"

"Plenty. We can't stay here. We can't fight an army. Let's get through the cabins and drop to the water on t'other side. They won't likely. . . ."

"Go ahead and save your skin, Parson." John grinned, teeth flashing white amidst his tangled black whiskers. "You're a man o' peace. But I ain't. I'm a fightin' man, and I wouldn't miss this here ruckus for all the Bibles in Boston."

"Then I won't run out, either!" the Parson announced. "I don't reckon it's too un-Christian to fight a gang o' varmints." He jerked a pistol from the band of his pants and waved it around in his vulture-claw hands. "I reckon we'll get killed doin' this, but we can die happy, knowin' it's been in a good cause."

"Ho-ho!" roared Comanche John, doing some polka steps in his heavy jackboots. "You may aim on gettin' killed, but not me. Don't forget what that Gypsy told me about passin' away rich and respected, a country squire betwixt snow-white sheets."

VI

Cutter and his men fanned out and advanced in the deep shadow cast by the decks. John's eyes became hard as he weaved from side to side, trying to pick out a subject for his marksmanship. One of Cutter's men blazed away at the boat. Like an echo, John's right hand Navy barked. There was a cry, and they could hear a horse splashing off through the water. They waited.

"Wish they'd hurry up about it," complained John. "Seems to be takin' 'em an unnatural long time."

The parson thought the same. Several men were riding around, shouting, cursing, but they were making no attempt to come aboard. John raised up to get a view of the river over the bow of the boat. He caught sight of shadowy forms moving quietly around to the other side of the boat.

"Parson, they're aimin' on takin' us from behind."

Nearby were stairs leading up to the hurricane deck. They were in shadow, but strong moonlight covered the deck. A look-out on the shore raised a cry and cut loose with a Henry rifle. Comanche John flung himself face foremost to the hurricane deck as the bullet ripped splinters.

The parson climbed up and stood there in full sight. He didn't seem to know where the bullets were coming from. John dragged him to the deck. There, in the partial shadow of the rail, they were momentarily safe. The hurricane deck extended three-fourths the length of the boat. It was unobstructed except for the small texas, the pilot house, and two smokestacks. Its boards were scrubbed white so the moonlight reflected as from snow.

"What we waitin' for?" asked the parson.

"Can't you see? There's a man, yonder with a Henry rifle. If we cross over to the texas, it'll have to be on the lope. Ready?"

"I ain't backed up yet, have I?"

John ran for it, with the parson loping behind. The Henry rifle *whanged,* encouraging them to speed. Once inside the texas they were protected, and they had an unobstructed view of the deck, but there was no escape except above to the pilot house, and from the pilot house there was no escape at all.

"Trapped here like two rats!" fumed the parson accusingly.

But John seemed unworried. "Mebby, but these two rats are the kind which spit right in the trapper's eye."

The shouting had died. In its place came only a murmur of voices. Now and then a horse splashed. An almost imperceptible vibration of the boat told them that men were climbing aboard and moving along the deck. Comanche John tried to keep watch of both sides of the texas at once. The parson, who had taken time to poke through the captain's stateroom, came out with a nickel-plated sawed-off shotgun, a patent powder horn and cap box, and a pouch of buckshot.

"Parson, that's just the gun for a marksman like you. I was a mite worried before, but I ain't now."

"Listen!"

Someone had crawled onto the hurricane and was now wriggling across, trying to keep in the shadow of a smokestack. The parson raised his shotgun, but John held him back. "Wait thar, Parson. There's somethin' unusual about that lad."

Suddenly the man hopped to his feet and ran toward the texas at a hunched-over gallop. Two or three guns sent out streaks of fire from the edge of the deck. John flung open the door, and the fellow came in. It was the Negro boy who had been firing the boilers.

He pointed and rolled the whites of his eyes: "Dey was a-goin' to wreak vengeance on me. Cap'n Cutter, he was goin' to carve on me wit' his knife. Said I helped you out. I said no, dat you'd kilt me if I'd of crossed you. He cussed and said I was a run-away nigger, but dat ain't true. De gov'mint man said I was freed. He say all us niggers was free men now dat de Nawth says we're free."

"Don't look like none of us is free, what with that Cutter and his gang on every side," John said sourly. He wasn't an Abolitionist like the parson, and the thought of a freed slave was too much for his digestion. But in spite of that he sympathized with the boy. He said: "Don't worry about him carvin' you. Here, take this Texas Derringer. Each o' them bar'ls is loaded with an ounce of buck, so you won't have to shoot too accurate. Just wait till they get inside tobacco-juice distance and whang away."

The parson muttered something and let fly with his sawed-off. That seemed to be the spark that set off the fireworks. A dozen guns roared out. The glass of windows splintered and tinkled to the floor while stinging fragments of it filled the air. The parson blasted with the second barrel, and then fumbled around trying to reload in the dark.

"Steady, Parson," said John. "They're only tryin' to get us to empty our weppons."

"Don't reckon that critter wants any more weapons emptied at him," the parson responded.

John chuckled and let fly with a spurt of tobacco juice. "Parson, if you'd took to shootin' ruther than Bible shoutin', you might have ended up a real credit to the Nor'west."

"Hush up," hissed the parson. He had heard something suspicious. A second later he spied a form slipping along the deck, keeping within the shadow cast by one of the smokestacks. The parson leveled his sawed-off.

"Save it," grunted John. "He's only a decoy."

The boy pulled John's sleeve: "Please, Mist' John. I heered somethin' 'way back in de texas, yondah. You don't suppose . . . ?"

"Maybe it was witches." John grinned.

"Naw, sir, it warn't no witches. Laws, ain't any old witch make de floor squeak in walkin'. These was men, and I heered 'em."

They listened. Indeed, something was squeaking at the far end of the texas. Soon after, the squeaking sound was replaced by the sharp ripping of wood.

"They're comin' up through the floor!" John roared.

He started down the cross hall. Somebody shot, but it was dark and the bullets missed. John set himself, a Navy in each hand. He filled the darkness with flame and streaking lead. For a few seconds the attackers tried to make a stand of it, then they rolled back, falling over each other in the forward door.

It was a diversion—all that Cutter needed. From the other direction, his men came swarming across the deck. John could get rapid, moonlit flashes of their moving forms from the windows of the texas.

"Keep away from that door, Andy, you fool!" a coarse voice bellowed just outside.

But Andy paid no heed. He rushed on, flung open the door, poked a gun inside, and fired blindly. The firing was cut off suddenly as he met the lead from Comanche John's left-hand Navy.

"Yip-ee!" roared John. "This is the life for me. Come on, you sea-goin' polecats, I still got bullets for a six of ye!"

"John? Is that you?" It was the parson. He sounded delirious. "Where are we? What's goin' on?"

The parson staggered to his feet. He saw the door and went toward it. John shoved him away just in time. A bullet whipped through into the far wall. The parson had tried to stay erect on his wobbly old legs, but John had not pushed him gently, and he backpedaled to collapse against a far wall.

"Whar's my shotgun?" he moaned, feeling around the floor. "John, you help me find my shotgun so's I can shoot the buzzards."

"Lay low, Parson, I'm cleanin' 'em out satisfactory."

"Yes, sah!" exclaimed the Negro lad. "Mist' John is sho-nuff potent with the pistols."

It became suddenly silent. Everyone was lying low. The deck seemed to be deserted. John stood there, reloading the empty cylinders of his Navies—a slow job in the dark. He could hear the parson muttering as he felt along the floor for his sawed-off. Footsteps—overhead on the texas roof. He listened for a minute or so, then they hurried away.

Cutter's voice: "Get down. Do you want to get half a steel hoop through your skull? I've lost too many men already."

"Half a hoop?" John muttered. "What the thunder? Say, let's get out of here. Sounds like they've set a keg o' powder on the roof."

But as he spoke, the explosion hit them. The concussion of it cracked the texas wide open. Its front and part of one side was flung across the deck. The air was blinding with smoke and burning powder pellets and wood fragments. John was on his knees amid the wreckage. He called the parson's name, but there was no answer. He felt his way over fallen timbers to the forward end of the texas. The pilot house was still intact. He saw the ladder and made it up there to escape Cutter's men who were coming from every direction. The pilot house door was open. He went inside. One of his guns was down below—the other only had a couple of shots left in it. He fumbled with it in the dark.

"Hank?" It was Captain Cutter's voice.

Cutter seemed to recognize Comanche John the same moment he spoke. It was too close for pistols. They grappled. It was an even balance of weight and strength. They plunged back and forth in the tiny room.

Cutter suddenly released his grip and spun away. He was familiar with the lay-out of the pilot house, and John wasn't. He ducked beneath the deck and came up on the other side. John glimpsed the glimmer of pistol steel in his hand. He reached for his Navy, but the holster was empty. The gun had been lost somewhere in the dark.

He flung himself against the wall as the bullet whisked by. He dived for the floor as Cutter located him for a second shot. A third bullet tore splinters from the floor between John's cheek and his outstretched hand. He came up to a crouch and drove forward, smacking Cutter in the midsection and causing a fourth bullet to go wild through the roof.

Cutter doubled his knee, trying to sink it into John's abdomen. He let it go like an uncoiling spring. John was knocked away, but not hurt. He roared, swallowed his tobacco, and charged again.

Cutter went for a strangle hold, but that was a mistake. John caught him with a ripping elbow blow. The strangle hold was loosened, and Cutter hit the wall. John nailed him as he rebounded. It was a right, perfectly timed. Cutter went to his knees. John lifted him, and smashed home another. Cutter whispered: "Don't. In the name of God, don't."

John was going for his coat collar to drag him back, but Cutter wriggled away in the dark. He made it to the door, and half fell, half leaped to the hurricane deck below. John followed a second later. He looked around, but Cutter had found some place of concealment. Men loomed from every side. He turned to escape, but something struck him. His eyeballs burst with a dazzle of light, and then everything dissolved in a swirl of darkness.

When John came to, he was on his back. He raised his aching head to look around. He propped himself on his elbows. There were men gathered around him, but it took him a while to make out who they were.

"Hi, Cap'n," said John to Cutter who stood eight or ten feet away. "Are you aimin' we should finish our duel here and now? I knowed you was a Southern gent'man like myself and wouldn't best a man except in fair, square combat. What weppons are we a-goin' to use?"

Cutter laughed. It wasn't a pleasant laugh. It was the kind of laugh that grinds one's nerves like sandy bread grinds teeth. Cutter took one step forward. John could see moonlight glimmer on the pistol he held.

"Why, we'll each use the weapons we have." Cutter smiled.

John sat up, his eyes taking stock of his predicament. The texas wall was on one side. Cutter's men formed a semicircle around him with drawn guns.

"Yes"—Cutter smiled—"it is true I am a gentleman of the Old South and, that being the case, I will deal with you the way your class should be dealt with. We do not duel with white trash. We merely do away with them when they become too obnoxious."

Cutter paused and listened. From down below came the sound of popping boiler rivets. The odor of burning grease was heavy on the night air. Overhead, clouds of dark smoke still rolled from the twin smokestacks. He started to speak, then paused again, his eyes on a form that was struggling toward them.

In a moment they could make out a man, dragging himself painfully. It seemed that his legs were paralyzed, and only his arms had the power of locomotion. He was trying to speak, but his voice did not carry.

"What the devil?" said Cutter.

"It's Stenson, the engineer!" one of his men shouted. "A bullet got him through the legs."

Stenson came on for a few yards, then he paused. He rolled to support himself on one hand and gestured toward the engine room. "The boilers! They can't last much longer! The safety valve . . . he . . . that Comanche John . . . he roped the anvil to it. . . ."

Cutter took a quick stride toward Comanche John. In the next second, the deck rocked and leaped beneath them. For a time they seemed caught in the midst of a mighty exhalation. Then the craft parted in her middle, hurling her insides toward the sky with a mounting, tumultuous roar.

Comanche John came to and found himself sprawled in the V formed by the sloping deck and the wall of the texas. It had been only a second or two since the explosion, for the air was dense with steam and flame, and the wrecked hulk was strongly on the lurch.

Cutter was over there on hands and knees, looking at him. His gun had been knocked from his hand. He looked around. By the flame of burning timbers he spotted it, wedged among some torn boards of the deck. He made for it, but one of his men staggered up, blocking the way. Cutter cursed and shouldered him aside. The man was half groggy, and he fell. A Navy revolver in the man's holster was only a long reach from Comanche John's hand.

John pounced on it just as Cutter turned. The two guns sounded almost in unison, but one of them was first. Comanche John's bullet was a fraction of a second ahead.

Cutter staggered with the lurch of the boat. He hit the deck headfirst and lay still.

John made it to his feet. He took a step just as the hull, its explosion-born swell ridden out, hit bottom with a grinding crash. John went down from the impact, and the timbers of the burning pilot house pinned him.

He struggled, but he might as well have tried to free himself from the jaws of a bear trap. After a time he lay and rested. Below he could hear the whisper of water as it flowed through the sunken staterooms and another sound, not so restful—the swiftly accelerating crackle of burning wood.

Ross MacLain and his men waited at Assiniboine Coulée until after midnight. When one o'clock passed with no sign of Cutter or the *White Cloud*, he sent one of his men to a high bluff for a look up and down the river. In ten minutes the look-out came down, pushing his horse at a gallop. He had sighted the flames of a steamboat's pitch baskets five or six miles upstream. The boat, he said, was not moving.

Ross ordered his men up the bluffs, and they covered the distance swiftly. They drew up at the edge of the bench and looked down at a boat apparently aground. Through the night air came the crackle of gunfire.

He led the way down the bluffs. There was no trail, and the horses picked their way cautiously. Without warning, the steamboat seemed to lift herself from the water, and she burst with a roar and clouds of enveloping steam.

The steam drifted away like fog across the water. The boat came to sight after a quarter minute, listing and settling into the channel. Fires spread from the shattered furnaces and broke out along the decks.

Ross drove his horse on and was at the shore when the first of the survivors came splashing in. Cutter's men, and they had little fight left.

"Mist' Ross!"

Ross located the voice. It belonged to a Negro boy who worked for Cutter. "Here I am, Cletus."

"Mist' Ross, Comanche John and de preacher man is still on de boat, yondah. Dey saved de ol' *White Cloud*, but I'm scairt dey's daid now. I jumped in de watah an' 'spec' de preacher is goin' to follow, but I nevah see him no mo'."

"You mean they're alive . . . on board?"

Ross splashed his mount into the water, but one of his men seized the bridle. "You can't save them now. Look at those decks."

"Save who?"

It was the parson. He was wading toward the bank through water up to his waist—wading slowly because of some hulk he was dragging behind. "I reckon this accounts for all that's worth accountin' for," he said, panting from his exertion. "Yep, gaze upon Comanche John. He's a trifle scorched around the whiskers, but it's a light singe compared with what he'll get in the hereafter if he don't mend his ways."

John shook water from his whiskers and sat up in the mire near shore. He had a wild gleam in his eyes. "You over thar on the stagecoach!" he boomed. "Git yore hands up! Share and share alike is my motto!"

The parson splashed water on his face. "John! You ain't holdin' up no coach. You're here, fetlock deep in the Missouri."

"Parson? Is that you? Thunderation! Don't tell me you rescued me! Laws! . . . Comanche John bein' rescued by a sky pilot! It would be just like one o' my enemies to make up a verse about it."

Half an hour later, when they had dried off a little and

were headed toward camp, Ross said: "I don't know how I'll ever make it up to you two men."

John grinned. "You had ort to hire the parson yonder as a pilot."

Ross said: "There's a girl back in camp I have a question to ask, and, if I'm as lucky as I think I am, the parson will first have to perform a marriage ceremony. After that, he can have the best job on the river. And you, too, John."

"Would you make me a captain?"

"You bet I would!"

John scratched his damp whiskers. "Waal, I could get me Whisky Anderson for mate, and Three-Gun Guffy for second mate, if they ain't been hung. By the way, Ross, I wouldn't be surprised if a pirate boat could do considerable well for herself, long around clean-up time at the mines."

War Bonnet Ambush

I

The wagon train creaked wearily through the sultry hours of that August afternoon. To the south and east were unending plains. In the northwest were mountains, purple from distance, and in the sky, rising and rising until it faded in a smudge of gray, was a war signal of the Sioux. At sundown another signal smoke answered, then another, and another, each at greater distance.

The scouts rode far ahead, watching for Sioux, but none of those wild riders of the plains was visible, only their "smokes that talked." Bullwhackers, usually voluble, became grim and silent, letting their long whips speak for them. Mothers watched with worried faces from the backs of pitching Conestoga wagons, and, when evening came, there was extra caution shown in making the circle.

Jack Sells, tall and raw-boned, with eyes and temper as sharp as the teeth of a saw, inspected the circle with a swift glance, then he coiled his long bullwhip and mounted his chestnut horse.

"What's up?" asked a flat-faced half-breed called Blackfoot.

"That damned parson over there. He's making trouble again."

"I'd wring his rooster neck," growled Alvis Tucker.

Blackfoot, Tucker, and a snaggle-toothed trapper named Lesh had come with Sells from Fort Landen.

"You stay back, and keep your hands away from your guns. We have to treat these Missouri farmers easy for a day or two. I'll manage the parson."

Sells rode across to Cy Denton's wagon. Cy was a man of middle height and middle years. The parson was a straggly-whiskered old scarecrow. It was the parson who had organized this wagon train of farmers back on the Platte. He had intended to take them on the southern route by way of Jim Bridger's fort, but Sells and his men had joined up near Laramie and sold them on the advantages of the shorter route to Fort Landen. Sells owned Fort Landon and traded fresh mules for worn-out mules at the rate of one for three, and it was his practice to act as guide when a big outfit like this one came along.

Sells rode up to where the parson was talking vehemently to Denton, and swung down, reaching for the ground with a powerful leg. He walked over, dragging the heels of his dusty horsehide boots, massive shoulders hanging loose, his rolled-up bullwhip in his hand. "What the hell, Parson?" he asked, trying to show that he was really a fine fellow in spite of his rough exterior. "You aren't gettin' scared of them squaw fires, are you?"

"Those aren't squaw fires!" the parson cackled in his rooster voice. "I know war signals when I see 'em. I been in this country before, Sells. I been up the Oregon Trail, the way this wagon train should be goin'. The way it *would* be goin', if I'd had my way."

Sells looked at him contemptuously, then he turned his back to talk to Denton. "You're not taking this Bible shouter seriously, are you?"

Denton rubbed the gray stubble at his chin. "Damn it, Sells, those signal smokes . . . I don't know much about Indians, but I've always heard. . . ."

"I'll get you through, just as I promised."

"There are women and children along, Sells. I don't. . . ."

"I said I'd get you through!"

The parson was bristling like a fighting cock. "Yes, you'd risk the necks of everybody here just so's we'd go to your fort instead of Bridger's. Just for the sake of trading a few mules!"

Sell's hand closed, massive and brown, on the coiled whip. He could use that whip as other men could use a gun. In his hand it was fast, accurate, and deadly. There were plenty of stories along the trail about how he had snapped men's necks with that whip. Judging by the fury in Sell's eyes, he would have snapped the parson's neck had not Denton and the others been around to watch. Sells spoke, his voice trembling a little from the anger he was trying to hold down. "I've let you get away with a lot of talk these last few days, Parson. On account of that gray hair. But don't shove me too far."

The parson paid no attention. "They told us back in Fort Laramie that the Sioux were war pathin'. Let's call a confab tonight and talk it over. You go see Bender and some of. . . ."

"I suppose you want to turn around and go back," Sells sneered.

"No, but we can still turn south. Right yonder, alongside the mountains. We can make it over to Bridger's."

A red-whiskered, heavy-jawed man stalked up after unsnapping his string from his tandem wagons. "You causin' trouble again?" he grunted, scowling at the parson.

"Listen here, Bender, I'm tryin' to save our hides . . . yours and your womenfolk's and kids' as well as everybody else's. Sells, here, is takin' us through war country just for the sake of tradin' a few mules and gettin' what money we have for supplies."

Sells's fury finally got the better of him. He'd taken more from this ornery old sky pilot than he'd taken from any man in his life. Veins stood out on his forehead. The muscles of his arms tightened the sleeves of his blue linsey shirt. He strode forward, expecting the parson to retreat, but the parson was not the retreating kind. He grabbed the old fellow and spun him as though he were light as a straw-filled scarecrow.

"Are you tryin' to say I'm in with the Injuns?" he bellowed.

"No. But, if I thought it, I'd say it. You're for yourself, first, last, and day after tomorrow. You'll take us through, if it's handy, and ride for your life if it ain't. I never said it before, because it ain't my habit to go around ruining men's reputations behind their backs, but you ain't especially high regarded along the trail. You've taken trains into the bad places before, and then got out with your own hide. Two, three year ago when I was ridin' up from Salt Lake. . . ."

There was too much truth in this for Sells to take. He thrust the parson back, and struck him with the heel of his right hand. The blow would have staggered a mule, and the parson struck the dirt shoulder first like so many loosely tied bones. He lay still with Sells looming over him, trembling with the desire to plunge on and swing his heavy boots.

"Jack!" cautioned Alvis Tucker who had ridden up behind him.

Sells breathed out deeply and shook himself. He had to hold back. The parson had friends among these hay shakers. They were new to the country—didn't understand the frontier, how men fought. Just a day or two more of going easy, then he didn't give a damn. They'd have to go on to Fort Landen, regardless.

The parson lay stretched out quite still for eight or ten seconds while blood ran from the corner of his mouth. Bender and Denton stood silently staring at him.

The cry of a woman broke the trance-like quality of the

scene. A girl of nineteen or twenty ran down the rear steps from Denton's wagon, holding her long calico dress up from her moccasined feet. She threw herself beside the parson and took his gray head in her lap. "Parson! Oh, Parson. . . ."

He was alive. He commenced rolling his head around on the end of his scrawny neck.

Her fear left her then, and anger showed in its place. She stood up, looking at Sells with contempt, then at Denton, and the red-whiskered Bender. "You let him do this! You just stand there and. . . ."

"Mary, my child." Cy Denton walked toward his daughter. "You don't understand. . . ."

"You mean you'd stand by and let him do this to the parson? To this poor old man?" She turned on Sells. "Oh, I know how you've fooled Bender and most of the others. . . ."

"Mary! Go back to the wagon!" her father commanded.

A dozen men had gathered by that time, and more were on their way. Her eyes picked one of them out. He was a tall, rather lanky lad with a good jaw and intelligent, blue eyes. "Steve! See what they've let him do to the parson. . . ."

The parson sat up, shaking his ancient head. He revolved his jaw slowly, muttering.

Steve bent over him and shook his shoulder. "Parson, are you hurt?" The parson could only mutter.

Mary pointed to Sells who stood looking at them with truculent eyes.

Steve faced him, trembling a little from anger. "Did you hit the parson?" he asked.

Sells laughed. "Well, now, if it isn't little Stevie James, showin' off for the lady!" His assumed smile suddenly vanished, and he barked: "Yes, I hit him! I slapped him, anyhow, though I dare say he's putting on an act to get sympathy right now. There are some things a man can't take, not even from a graybeard."

Steve started forward, but Bender grabbed his arm. "Here! I'm head o' this train, and I say no fightin'. You may not agree with Sells, but we took him on as guide, and it's up to us to abide by what he says. Even if. . . ."

Steve jerked away. Sells was still there, hands on hips, whip rolled, grinning through tobacco-stained teeth. His attitude was a challenge for the younger man to fight.

Steve swung a left and followed with a right. The force of those blows surprised Sells a little. He shook himself, roared, and sprang forward, his left arm swinging in a devastating arc. The blow caught Steve high on the cheek and smashed him so that he sprawled far back on the ground. Sells started forward as though to give him the boots, but he stopped suddenly. He thought Steve was going for the Navy revolver at his hip.

Actually the gun had only been knocked loose from its holster by the fall. Sells carried a pistol at each hip, but he did not reach for them. He owned a faster weapon. He swung his long bullwhip quick as a striking snake. The lash wrapped around Steve's right wrist.

Sells reared back, snapping Steve to his feet. He relaxed the whip so it unwound. He swung it back over his shoulder. Mary screamed and started forward, but the whip cracked like a rifle in front of her, making her draw back.

Sells laughed and said: "Don't worry about your sweetheart, little gal. I ain't a-goin' to kill him. No, I just want to demonstrate some of my tricks . . . tricks I save up for buckos who try to draw guns on me."

The next swing of the whip caught Steve on the right shoulder, tearing a fragment from his blue shirt and starting blood to oozing. Steve was still groggy. He staggered and went to his knees, lips contorted from pain.

Sells said: "And, now, Stevie my lad, just so's you won't hear too much and get yourself into so much trouble, I'm goin' to have one of your ears for a souvenir."

Mary screamed. Her father held her back, but took a step forward himself. "Sells!" he shouted.

Bender got his bull voice to going: "Let him go, Denton! It'll teach the young fool a lesson."

"Oh, ho!" chortled Alvis Tucker, slapping the pommel of his Mexican saddle in appreciation of Bender's judgment.

Steve didn't know quite what was going on. His hat was off; his blondish hair blew in the slight evening breeze so that his right ear was revealed. It would be the whip of the master that could snap off that ear. Sells stood with shoulders high, legs planted. He recoiled the whip and hefted it a second. He threw back his arm, allowing the lash to roll out behind him. He bent forward, and the long lash followed. But, instead of a pop of the lash, a gun roared out. The whip and part of the stock sailed through the air, slapping harmlessly against a high wheel of the Conestoga wagon near which Steve crouched.

Sells hung there a second, not realizing what had happened. He stared at the whip stock, severed just above his hand by a bullet. Then he spun around.

An unkempt, black-whiskered stranger sat in slouched indolence on a wiry, Nez Percé pony a dozen long strides away. In his hand was a Navy pistol with a wisp of powder smoke stringing up from the muzzle. He wore a floppy black hat, a Cree jacket with most of its beadwork missing, homespun pants, and scuffed jackboots. The man chewed for a while, watching with deceptive drowsiness from beneath drooping eyelids. Then he spat tobacco juice and said: "Now, what was you sayin' about an ear?"

"Where'd you come from?" barked Sells.

"Me? Why I come from a whole heap of a distance off. But back to that ear. I ain't sayin' I'm exactly the man that can pluck one off with a long lash, though I have done a bit o' bullwhackin'. But with a Navy pistol, now . . . you take that right ear of yourn, for example. . . ."

"Comanche John!" It was the parson. He had recovered and was now advancing on his rickety legs. "Why, I heered they'd hung you up in Virginny City."

"Yipee!" John slid his Navy back in its tied-down holster, and reached for earth with one jackboot. "Parson, how are the sinners? I heered you was guidin' a wagon train for I-dee-ho, but I never suspected you'd be so thin-brained as to pick this Fort Landen route. Why, I supposed you'd be headed for Bridger's place, two, three days to the south."

Comanche John shook the parson's hand so violently the bony old man was almost jerked from his feet. He seemed to have forgotten all about Sells and the others, although a careful observer might have noticed that the butt of his right-hand Navy was always in the clear.

"You mean you came south just lookin' for me?" asked the parson.

"Yep." John twisted his whiskers around and spat tobacco juice with disapproval. "Oh, them gold camps! They're wicked. Plumb wicked. To shame. Sody and Gomorrah, as you say in your sermons. I don't want no more part of 'em, Parson. Why, you know what them ring-tailed rangy-tangs up in Bannack tried to do to me? They tried to give me a pree-sentation. A cravat. Guaranteed to hold a man's weight and last him a lifetime. Even offered to tie a knot in it for me. But you know how I am, Parson. Never the one to accept gifts. I says . . . 'No, boys, you just keep your blamed cravat. I'm ridin' southwise'."

The parson pulled Comanche John away so he'd be sure no one could overhear. "John, you ain't done it again? You ain't gone back to coach robbin' after all the reformin' I done on you."

John whacked dust from the leg of his homespun pants and guffawed. "Why, share and share alike is my motto, and I'd call that to be a Christian atty-tude."

"Should have known you'd never get to be an honest man," said the parson sadly. "I always liked you, John, but heaven help me, if I was sittin' on your jury when you came up, I think I'd vote to condemn you. You'll never in all your life sway from the paths of skullduggery and wretchedness."

"Hell, Parson, don't take it so hard." He went on impressively. "Guess you don't know what a personage I'm gettin' to be. They even made up a song about me. Want to hear it?"

"I have heard it."

"Yes, but maybe not the newest verses. Why, every muleskinner on the road from Salt Lake to Bannack has made up a verse. Listen to this one. It's about me robbin' that Yuba coach down in Californy. . . ." And John commenced singing in a frog-like voice.

Comanche John rode out with a lad
By the name of Cisco Bill,
They stopped that six-horse Yuba coach
At the top of Lone Pine Hill. . . .

"You ain't makin' it any easier on me by lettin' 'em know you're a road agent," snapped the parson.

John chewed for a while, looking searchingly at the parson, and then at all the suspicious faces. "What's gone wrong in this pilgrim string, anyhow?"

"There's aplenty that's wrong."

"How'd you come by that bruise alongside your head?"

"Never mind."

"How'd you git it?" John was not bantering now. His voice had a whipsaw note in it. His eyes were hard as twin pieces of quartz.

"I ain't startin' no more trouble than we got already," said the parson. "How I got this bruise is my affair, and I'm willin' that bygones should be bygones. I reckon the Sioux will give us all the trouble we need without any help."

John let his bridle reins drag while he slouched forward to face Sells. Sells had recovered his arrogance by now and stood with his stud-horse legs spread far apart, his thumbs hanging in his crossed gun belts. At one side of him, mounted, sat the half-breed, Blackfoot, with a rifle across his pommel. On the other side was Alvis Tucker, hawk-faced and intent, and Lesh, a dirty, bleary whisky soak and frontier renegade. Around about were others—muleskinners, honest farmers, come West looking for a home and now scared half out of their wits by Sioux war signals. There were women and kids with faces poked from the ends of canvas-topped wagons —John saw these, too.

Sells barked: "We know who you are, and we don't want any of your kind. You're a road agent. You're Comanche John. You weren't keeping it a secret by all your hush-down talk. You were run out of Californy, and out of Idaho, and probably out of Montana Territory, if the truth was known."

John laughed, looking around at the tattered wagons and the played-out stock. "I 'low this would be one devil of a spot for a stagecoach robber."

"Move on!" shouted Sells. "Git on to the south while you're still healthy!" He was speaking with his old-time swagger now that his men were in position to back him.

John chewed slowly, rubbing his whiskers with a

thoughtful hand. "Mebby I will, and then mebby I won't. It all depends on the parson, yonder. He's my shepherd, sort of. But whether I do or I don't, I'm goin' to say what I rode in here to say. And here she is . . . there's Injuns war pathin' all the way north to Montana country. They've burned every trapper's cabin and immigrant wagon betwixt the Sulphur Water and Fort Landen. They're wild, them Injuns, wrought up because they see white men rollin' in by thousands, shootin' off the buffalo, and plowin' under the grass. So far it's been only the Sioux and the Crows. The Cheyennes are still peaceful as they usually are, which ain't sayin' a heap. If you get south to Cheyenne country, you should be able to make it on to Fort Bridger. You can stop thar and wait till the government gets soldiers up from Salt Lake."

Sells tossed back his head and laughed derisively. "Go south to Fort Bridger . . . two hundred miles out of our way? And with Fort Landen almost in sight across that little range of mountains?" He looked at Comanche John, twisting down the corners of his wide, thick-lipped mouth. "Just what sort of a game are you playing, anyhow?"

John didn't bother to answer. He chuckled as though he found something amusing about the whole thing and slouched over toward the wagon where most of the bullwhackers had gathered.

"Who's the head of this outfit?" he asked.

Bender came forward, his red whiskers fairly bristling with importance. "I am."

"What do you aim to do?"

"I aim to cross the mountains to Fort Landen, of course."

"Ain't the parson your guide?"

"Not any more he ain't."

John turned abruptly. "Then, Parson, maybe we better hit for the south. I ain't hankerin' that *my* hair should decorate some Sioux lodgepole."

Denton started explaining: "You see, stranger, we all have faith in the parson, but it's been six years since he was over the trail. Then Sells came along and offered to guide us to Fort Landen. . . ."

"Which he owns!" yipped the parson.

"Well, perhaps. Anyway, we voted, and now I don't think it would be a good idea to start south. But we still need the parson. We need him mighty bad to guide us from Landen to Idaho."

"Well, Parson, what she be?" John asked.

"I'm going to stay, John. I ain't the quittin' kind. You ride on if you like. . . ."

"And leave you here amongst these wolves? Reckon I can tolerate this sort of company if you can." He squinted over at Mary. "Reckon *some* of them ain't so bad!"

II

Comanche John asked no other permission to join the wagon train. He simply led his cayuse over to the parson's wagon where he gave him a good feed of Indian meal. Afterward, he went inside, took off his hot jackboots, and wiggled his toes in comfort while the parson stewed buffalo jerky and dumplings for supper. "He ain't goin' to take this on his hunkers," the parson said, pausing in his culinary efforts to poke fresh sagebrush inside the dinky "Daniel Boone" stove. "He ain't goin' to let you stay with this train if he can help it."

"You mean Sells? Reckon I'll take care of my own hide, Parson. If need be, I'll amble over thar and put a Navy slug right betwixt his eyes."

"That's just what I'm skeered of. They'll hang you, if you do it, John."

"Lots of folks has got it in their heads to hang me," said John placidly.

He was at the table, forking dumplings and jerky in his mouth, when feet thumped on the let-down steps of the wagon, and Steve James came in. He said: "I didn't get around to thanking you, but. . . ."

"Forget it," grunted John. "I always was the one to unlimber my Navy in the cause of decency and honor."

Steve paused in the door, his young brows drawn in a troubled line. He had changed his whip-torn shirt, and nothing except a bruise high on his cheek gave evidence of his recent engagement with Sells. "They're havin' a powwow over at Bender's wagon," he said.

"Concernin' me?"

"Yes."

"What's the verdict?"

"I don't know yet . . . but I don't doubt it would be safest to light out."

"Me? Comanche John? Light out?" He snorted, and shoveled dumplings with the razor-sharp end of his Bowie knife. "Ain't you heered the song they made up about me? Every muleskinner from Salt Lake to. . . ."

The parson cut in: "That song's goin' to be the ruin of you yet. You're like all badmen . . . you get yourself a fancy reputation and then try to live up to it. And do you know where that leads? It leads right smack under a cottonwood limb."

John grinned, and shoveled in more dumplings.

Steve said: "Seriously, Sells is out to get you. And he has Bender on his side. Bender is strong-headed and a damned fool in lots of ways, but he's honest, and all the others know it. They'll do pretty much what Bender wants."

John still seemed unperturbed, but his eyes were cold and speculative. He had risked his life in a hundred ways, but for all that he was not suicidal. He could shake a bush as fast as the next one when the necessity arose. "What, exactly, is he sayin' about me? That I was a road agent, and more such-like lies?"

"That, and more. He claims you and the parson made a deal . . . the parson was supposed to guide the train to some place south of here where you have a gang waiting. White men dressed up like Indians. He says that's why you came along . . . to scare them south."

John chewed for a while, then said: "Steve, you git back to that fire. I'll sort of keep my cayuse saddled, awaitin' developments."

After Steve left, the parson said: "You better do the high lope, John. This here's my party. If anybody's neck gets stretched, it ought to be mine."

"It ought," John conceded, "but likely it won't."

He stood near the back of the wagon, watching. Steve's tall silhouette could be made out near the fire. Bender was there—his broad, whiskered head and ponderous actions making him resemble a bull buffalo, and there was Sells and a lot more. Their fire had died to a heap of coals, and men could be seen wandering back toward their wagons, fagged after the trek and worry of the day. "Reckon I'm safe," yawned John. "The party seems to be breakin' up."

The night was quiet. No Indian sign. Nothing much happened the next day, either. Just the overloaded wagons rolling, kicking dust from the parched earth. Sells and his men stayed out in front, scouting for Indians. There were a couple of signal smokes, one at noon and one near sundown. The country became rolling, cut every half mile or so by deep, brush-filled coulées.

They camped in the middle of a wide swale. There were gullies, little hills, and brushy pockets around that would make excellent hiding spots for Indians, and no better place had been seen during the last hours. An air of tenseness was on the train—even more than the night before when there had been the excitement of Sell's bullwhip and Comanche John's Navy pistol.

Thunderclouds rolled up in the west. There was wind, and a few warm spatters of rain. Afterward a general grayness hung over the sky, hiding moon and stars. One by one the fires were killed, and the wagon circle lay in deep shadow with weather-drab tops invisible a short distance away. Scouts rode out their watches in a close circle. When John lay on his straw tick in the parson's wagon, he could hear the regular *thlot-thlot* of their horses' hoofs, blending with the little sounds from the nervous camp, and distantly the yapping of coyotes—or humans, giving a good imitation. John fell asleep and snored while the parson was still tossing around in his bunk.

Yet it was Comanche John who leaped awake, a Navy pistol in each hand. He had heard the first shout of "Indians!" He kicked his feet into his jackboots, buckled on his belts, and let himself down from the rear of the wagon. Still no moon or stars, not even the phosphorescent night glow that usually came from the horizon. In a moment, the parson piled down behind him, dragging an ancient flintlock rifle.

John said: "Take her ca'm, Parson, and quit hoppin' around like the pack rat that got lost in the roulette wheel. Stay behind that wagon wheel over yonder and don't shoot till you see the steel of their scalpin' knives. Do much runnin' around, and these Missouri hay shakers will likely shoot you for an Injun. I don't reckon most of 'em has been in battle before."

The camp was disorderly with excitement. Children wept as frantic women dragged them from bed to hide in the poor protection of trunks, bureaus, and what other junk they had carted from the old home. Men were running around with rifles and revolvers, letting their imagination see painted warriors in every direction. Somebody fired, itchy-fingered. A dozen others fired because of him, all bullets going wild into the surrounding dark. John grunted, got himself to one knee, and stuffed his cheek with blackjack tobacco.

"Parson, did I ever tell you about the time I was cornered by five hundred ragin' Blackfeet up on the Three Forks, when. . . ."

"Hush up!"

John crouched, chuckling and chewing on his blackjack. Over in the middle of the circle, herded stock was milling around. The sound of them mixed with the hoofs out there on the prairie. Two or three Indian rifles cut the darkness with streaks of orange light. A bullet clipped the ground somewhere, and hummed away. There was an answering rattle of gunfire from the circle.

Up till then, the Indians had been quiet. Now their wild cries broke out, seeming to come from all directions at once. It was hard to tell if the camp was surrounded or not. One of the scouts rode in beside the parson's wagon and hit the ground on the run, shouting—"White man! White man!"—so no one would shoot him for an Indian.

He came back and crouched near Comanche John. John could locate him by his heavy, excited breathing as he waited for the charge to swing closer.

"They were out there in that brushy draw," he said in a whisper. "They came crawlin' up on hands and knees. I almost rode over one of 'em. Then Johnson raised a shout, and I saw the others on their horses. Mighty near got me."

The Indians swung close, and then away again, according to the sounds. There was no way of telling through the dark. Not more than a dozen of them in that first group, John guessed. They were holding their fire, too, after that first flurry of shots, which was better than the wagon train was doing. Another group sounded close, galloping, and circled, then a glow of something out there. John recognized it. It was the light that came from coals that had been dropped in the bottom of a water-soaked buffalo quiver—another, and another of those lights, finally a half dozen of them.

There was a sparkle of fire as an untipped arrow was drawn from one of those quivers. It darted through the night, spiraling a trifle, breaking into flame. The burning arrow sailed inside the circle and burned itself out in the dry earth. The next one fell short. The next struck a wagon tongue with a shower of sparks, then two from closer range, each darting from sight through a cloth wagon top. They were quickly put out.

Darkness came again, and the whooping Indians were swinging closer. This time there was a whole shower of arrows. One of them twinkled past only a long arm's reach from John's cheek. A wagon top was blazing over to the right, then another.

The wagons were dry. They were like gunpowder in the heat of August. At first there were billows of flame from burning canvas. The fires seemed to die out for a moment with only the hoops on top burning, then the boxes would roar up. There was no saving them. Men cramped the front wheels and pushed them outside the circle.

Firelight reached across the rolling country, casting huge shadows, making prairie dog mounds look like hills and waist-high sage seem like groves of cottonwood. The night was filled with moving shapes—both real and imaginary. Shooting became intermittent. The Indians seemed to have vanished. Only the distant *thud* of their horses sounded. Comanche John chewed calmly, one shoulder against an iron wagon tire, a Navy pistol in each hand.

Unexpectedly there came a concerted *whoop* from fifty throats, and Indians were charging in from the night. They did not circle this time. They galloped straight down on the wagons. A fury of gunfire met them. Here and there a rider toppled, but others closed the gap. Comanche John whooped and came up with both guns rocking in his hands. His first two shots connected, smashing warriors from their mounts. The riderless horses came on, wild-eyed, digging dirt as they shied close and galloped around the circle. The parson blazed away with unknown results. At John's elbow, the grim-faced scout calmly downed one man, rammed a prepared load down the barrel of his rifle, and downed another.

At the next wagon, a muleskinner was cutting loose with buckshot, and his woman was adding to the total with an old horse-pistol. Some of the warriors swung aside from this sudden blast of lead. Five of them came on, headed for a break between the parson's Conestoga and the old, heavy-wheeled Pittsburgh next to it. They looked huge, grotesque, inhuman, their bodies streaked with vermilion and yellow, their decorated buffalo-hide shields flung high, their rifles carried in one hand.

One of the horses shied suddenly, throwing its rider. Another horse came on, making it over the wagon tongue. John was on one knee, both Navies blazing. The parson was on his hind legs, swinging his musket with its barrel in his hands.

"Hooray for the parson!" yipped John.

An unhorsed rider came up, screaming his war cry, tomahawk upraised. The parson wielded his musket on him, too.

The Indians were not in overwhelming numbers, and the back of their charge now seemed to be broken. Riderless horses galloped around the circle, eyes staring at the firelight. The Indians retreated into the darkness, keeping up an intermittent rifle fire. At last that died away. The battle was over.

"Thar she be," yawned John. "Nothin' like a bit o' action to stimulate the stomach. You don't suppose there's a dish of dumplings left, Parson?"

"Help yourself," said the parson, and ambled away on a round of the wagons to perform the duties of his divine calling, for there had been casualties in the number of whites as well as Indians.

Dawn came up with a grayness turning to yellow and pink. No sign of Sioux. The vast country stretched away in primeval silence. John inspected his Navies, thrust them back in their well-worn scabbards, and climbed to the wagon for some cold dumplings. Then he flopped down on the bunk and slept.

III

Comanche John felt a tremble of the wagon box and sat up. Sun was shining on the canvas top, filling the interior with light and morning heat. The parson, more hollow-eyed and drawn than usual, was looking at him through the door.

"Sleepin'," grunted the parson. "Sleepin', while I go around, viewin' scenes that would wring tears out of a dried apple."

John sat up and gave his tangled whiskers a good scratching. "You do the prayin', Parson, and I'll do the fightin'. We always got on pretty good thataway in the past."

"Reckon I do more fightin' than you do prayin'."

"May be."

"Old man Dudley just cashed in his chips . . . iron arrowhead right through the gizzard. His womenfolk are carryin' on considerable. That Fitch fellow got killed, too, but he was a bachelor, thanks be to goodness."

"They'd have been more of 'em if it hadn't been for my Navies," John growled defensively.

"Sure. Guess I don't mind if you slept. I'm just gettin' cantankerous in my old age." He sat down with his chin in his hands and slowly weaved from side to side. "Sometimes I think I'm not long for this world, John. And I hate to think what'll happen to you when I leave it."

"There's nothin' wrong with you that a cup of coffee won't cure." John sniffed the morning air. "And there's a smell of one from Denton's wagon, yonder."

John and the parson were having hot coffee poured by Mary Denton when her father came up the steps.

He said: "It's only fair for me to warn you two men that you're under considerable suspicion since last night's battle."

"Us?" yipped the parson.

"Yes. You and Comanche John, there."

John slammed the table with his fist. "There's some of your Christian gratitude for you, Parson! Some of your heavy prayin' church members, I'll wager. And after we went and beat back them Injuns practically double-handed."

"What's Sells sayin' about us?" asked the parson.

"Sells thinks you're in league with the Indians. Of course, he suggested that before, only this time there seems to be a little something to substantiate it."

"What?"

"There was a white man, painted up and dressed like an Indian, among those who got killed last night."

"That doesn't prove a thing," John said. "There are plenty of white renegades and half-breeds who have took up with the Injuns."

"Well, you know how Bender is. He's bellowing for your scalps already."

John got up, felt of his pistol butts, and walked down the steps. It was time for the wagon train to be kicking dust for Fort Landen, but only two or three of the immigrants had hitched up. All the men seemed to be gathered by Bender's wagon.

John ambled over that way, his disreputable black hat on the back of his head, the twin butts of his Navy sixes hung wide and low. He chewed slowly as he walked, humming a bit of tune. On reaching the edge of the gathering, he paused, and spat.

"Waal, what you accusin' me of this mornin'?" he asked. "Is it bigamy, hoss-stealin', or a connivance to keep wagon trains from tradin' their worn-out mules in Fort Landen at the disgraceful rate of three for one?"

Sells was over there, big and raw-boned, his rear against the high wheel of a Conestoga wagon, his foot propped on the axle behind him, his bullwhip coiled in his massive right hand. Blackfoot, the half-breed, was at one side, his face flat and expressionless. Alvis Tucker and the bewhiskered, dirty-toothed Lesh were on the other side where they would be most useful in case of an emergency.

John pretended not to notice. He stood there, slouched, his eyelids drooping. Bender came forward a step or two, shaking his big, reddish head like a bull bison, his voice sounding in a rumble. "There was a white man killed on the prairie last night. A white man dressed in Injun clothes and Injun paint."

"Maybe he was a Fort Landen Injun," drawled John.

Sells moved suddenly, his quick rage showing on his face, then he restrained himself.

Bender roared: "What do you mean?"

"Just what you think I mean . . . that it would be just as easy for Sells to connive with the Injuns as me. But you're wrong both ways from the eight spot. There ain't neither of us connivin' with the Injuns. Your whole blamed, sway-backed, busted-down outfit wouldn't be worth it."

One of the muleskinners—a runt with copper-colored face blotches—fired up at this insult. "Is that so! Well, we got plenty of beans along, and spuds, and seed wheat, and flour. Guess they'd be worth a pretty penny at the prices I hear about up in them hell-roarin' Montana gold towns."

"They'd be worth as much to Sells as they would be to me."

No one said anything for a moment. They all seemed to be thinking it over, even Bender. It wasn't going quite the way Sells had planned. That was plain on his long, horse-like face as he started to walk away from the wagon.

Alvis Tucker moved a step into the clear, his thumb hooked in his gun belt. Lesh and Blackfoot stayed where they were, alert and watchful.

John could see the deadfall that was being set for him, although he seemed as relaxed and indolent as ever. Sells was no match for him with a Navy, and he knew it. He would not go for his gun. He wouldn't try to swing the whip, either. As for Lesh, it would take a moment to toss that rifle barrel around. Blackfoot was powerful but clumsy, and more at home with a Bowie or tomahawk. It was Alvis Tucker he would have to watch like a hawk.

Sells spoke, his voice distinct enough for everyone in the circle to hear. "You framed this attack . . . you and your so-called parson. You're a dirty renegade and a thief. . . ."

"Why, them is fightin' words." John pursed his lips and let out a stream of tobacco juice, rolling up the alkali-white dust an inch or two from the toes of Sells's horsehide boots. "Yep . . . fightin' words."

He seemed to be only watching Sells, but Alvis Tucker was in the corner of his eye. He saw Tucker swing his arm loosely, recognized the little, quick tension of muscles that telegraphed the draw. There appeared to be nothing hurried about John's response. It was a movement—careless and easy, a hitch of the shoulder. He didn't even leave off his tobacco chewing. Yet a Navy pistol had appeared in his right hand. It seemed to hesitate a bare fraction of a second. It bucked and roared to life. John was still facing Sells, but his eyes were frozen on Alvis Tucker.

Tucker went forward on bent knees, and plowed face first into dirt and buffalo grass, his Navy spinning from his loose fingers. Blackfoot was on his toes, but he quickly raised his hands to show he was not going for his gun. Lesh was crouched forward, rifle poised at a forty-five degree angle. Sells, who had been set to draw, retreated a step—this, during the seconds that the shot rattled away and the sodbusters clawed for cover.

The parson ran up, shaking his wild gray hair. He drew up abruptly and stared at the limp form of Tucker. "John!"

"Yep, I did it. Me and my Navy. A clean case of self-defense, Parson. No more sinful than that clip on the head you fetched that Sioux warrior last night, so don't light up the fire and brimstone." John slid the Navy back in its low, tied-down holster, and ambled back toward the parson's wagon, never quite losing sight of the men around him.

An observer might have thought John was going to the wagon for a nap, or a bite of breakfast, but once inside all his slouching indolence left him. He fell to work rapidly, dumping Indian meal and jerky into a sack, replenishing his supply of powder and ball. "Share and share alike is my motto," he muttered as he helped himself liberally to the parson's stores.

He let himself down from the far side of the wagon and saddled his Nez Percé pony. Then he crouched down and watched from beneath the wagon. Bender was over there, bellowing and flinging his arms around like a Confederate orator. Apparently there was still plenty of time, so John fed his pony a hatful of Indian meal.

Mary came to the rear door of Cy Denton's wagon and shaded her eyes against the morning sun to watch what was going on. She saw John, and came over. She said: "I saw it all, and I don't blame you a bit. That Alvis Tucker . . . he's a killer. Steve heard that back in Fort Laramie, but none of the men would believe him."

"He ain't a killer no more."

She seemed worried. "They're going to cause trouble for you. I wouldn't be surprised if they wanted to . . . to. . . ."

"To hang me? Laws, gal, there's been a heap o' men with them kind of idees, but I still got one of the solidest necks betwixt here and Orofino."

Bender had left off orating. He hurried up the steps to his wagon. In a few seconds he came out, strapping on an extra pistol.

"Waal, now," muttered John. "I reckon this means good bye."

He put a jackboot in the stirrup and swung to his pony's back. One of the muleskinners caught sight of him and shouted. The muleskinner drew a heavy, double-barreled pistol and fired. The pistol was loaded with buck, and fifty yards was long range for its powder charge, but there was still plenty of sting left in the pellets. A couple of them struck the pony. He snorted and left the ground twisting. John tried to straighten him out for the open country.

Everyone seemed to be running in his direction. There were more shots. Even with the pony cavorting like he was, John could hear bullets buzzing like yellow jackets. The pony plunged around the wagon, tried to clear the tongue, knocked himself sidewise on the tree, and spilled John face foremost on the ground. John came up, dragging a length of harness around his shoulders. Three or four muleskinners were covering him.

"Stick up your hands!" roared Bender.

John looked into the barrels of several pistols. He lifted his hands, taking time to call that Nez Percé pony every swear word west of Tennessee.

An excited, gun-waving mob surrounded him. Bender's coarse voice could be heard over everybody's. He had a Navy in his hand and was gesturing with it. "There's the killer! We'll show him he can't shoot down one of our guides and git away with it! The low-down road agent! String him up, I say. . . ."

"Every man deserves a trial," the parson objected.

"To hell with a trial. What's the need o' wastin' all that time? We all seen him do it. What we want is justice, and fast justice, too. Winters, you go git that picket rope."

John whipped some dust from his homespuns and allowed himself to be prodded along by three bullwhackers who had taken over as guards.

"Sure you don't need some help tyin' the knot?" he asked of Bender. "Them Californy collars is tricky business."

Bender stopped, one hand on his hip, the other swinging the big pistol. "Maybe you don't think we'll go through with this hangin'?"

"Reckon you will, all right. But it's every condemned man's right to have a good, clean drop with a knot tied right and hooked up right. That's all I'm askin'."

"And that's what you'll get."

The parson was still remonstrating, but nobody would listen to him. Even Cy Denton stood to one side, looking severe. "Can't you do something?" wailed the parson.

Denton shook his head. "Maybe you didn't see it . . . he just drew his gun and shot that poor Tucker fellow right between the eyes. And why he did it, I can't guess. Tucker seemed to be a quiet fellow. He was standing there, not saying a word."

"Standin' over there drawing his gun to shoot John on the sly!"

"Why, he just barely got his hand on his gun."

"Sure, that's just how fast John is. He happened to see that skunk from the side of his eye, and. . . ."

But the parson might as well have been talking to the endless Western skies. No one would listen to him.

John kept his arms high while his guns were unbuckled and tossed over against a wagon wheel. He seemed to be at ease, watching while a hangman's knot was twisted up, while a wagon tongue was laid across the tops of two covered wagons, while a barrel was rolled out to make a drop.

Sells and his two remaining henchmen kept to one side, watching, letting the honest muleskinners and farmers do the work.

"Looks like you win, Sells." John chewed, lifting his hands in a sad gesture.

Sells moved away from the high wagon wheel where he was leaning and pulled himself to his magnificent six feet three. "It's a habit I got," he said smugly.

"Mighty fine habit. Might-ee fine!"

Comanche John sighed, and seemed to be resigned to this fate of his, but his eyes, beneath their drooping lids, were as hard and quick as ever. He could see his guns over there by the wagon wheel. It was about a dozen strides. His Nez Percé pony had calmed down and was tied to the wheel on the other side. But the three guards stayed alert, guns in their hands. He tried to edge over a little, but a muleskinner with a shot-loaded double-pistol drew down on him.

"Back where you was, Comanche John, and no funny business."

John seemed grieved. "I aim to git hung peaceful, as a man o' good character should."

The barrel was set up beneath the crosspiece now. The noose with its grotesque spiral knot was dangling. Back on the ground, a man was pulling the noose up to the right height.

The parson had disappeared. In a moment he came in sight down the back steps of his wagon, carrying his battered Bible. He paused a few steps away and intoned in a graveyard voice: "Short and full o' pain is the life o' man born o' woman!"

"Amen!" responded John.

The parson bowed to the others. "Will you kindly retire to a respectful distance so I can give this unfortunate condemned man some private consolation in these, his final moments upon the earth?"

A trifle awed by the sincere sadness of the parson's manner, the guards commenced to obey. Sells was suspicious. He cried: "This is some sort of a trick!"

Over by the hangman's barrel somebody shouted: "Look out! He's got a pistol back of his. . . ."

But the parson, using his Bible as a blind, had drawn the pistol and now held it in his hand. It was an old-time horse pistol with a barrel large as a four-bit piece. Its hammer was cocked, and the parson's finger was crooked around the trigger. His arm shook as though with chills. "I ain't much of a marksman," he informed them in a mild voice, "but a man don't need to be with a scatter-gun and two ounces of squaw shot. Make a move and, so help me, I'll blast the spinal backbones right out of ye. Drop them guns!"

Nobody had ever seen the parson like this. His sincerity was beyond doubt. There was a saying—"Never argue with a woman or an armed preacher." The guards dropped their guns, and lifted their hands for good measure. Sells started forward, but the parson drew a bead on him, and he dug his boots in an abrupt stop. John galloped toward the wheel where his Navies lay.

All this took only a few seconds. It was ridiculous—one old man against all of them. The short, copper-freckled muleskinner ducked out of sight and came up with a pepperpot pistol in his hand. Just then Steve James rode up, leading an extra horse. He glimpsed the freckled man, drew, and fired. Steve probably had aimed to kill, but his bullet went low, smashing through the fellow's leg and knocking him to the ground beneath the wagon.

John snatched up his belts, drawing one of the guns. There was no doubt about the command of the situation then. Steve nudged his horse between the wagons, untied the Nez Percé, pony and led him out. John tossed the belts over the saddle horn and mounted without taking his intent eyes off the crowd. The parson got on the spare horse. The three rode slowly between the wagons.

No sound was made during these moments except for the little *crunch* of buffalo grass beneath hoofs and the *tinkle* of bit chains. There was a general exhalation when they passed out of sight.

Hoofs *thudded* in a sudden gallop. Bender commenced to shout. He leaped between the wagons, drawing his pistol. Comanche John wheeled in his saddle and aimed a bullet that sent him clawing for cover.

Sells bobbed down beneath the wagon box, firing and cursing, long after the men were beyond range of both voice and bullet lead. He stood up, and commenced pushing loads into the chambers of his pistols. After a while the signs of anger left his face, and he began looking satisfied with himself. After all, wasn't it better the way it had turned out? Hadn't he ridded himself of three troublemakers in one batch? Now, if the Sioux would hold off for three or four days, until he could nurse this creaking outfit with its half-dead stock to Fort Landen. . . . Sells walked away, making plans for that deal. He'd be tougher than usual this time. The train couldn't go on to Idaho without fresh stock. He'd demand four mules for one. That would mean some of the wagons would be left behind. He'd fat up the stock on that good Landen Valley grass, repair the wagons, and trade them at the gold camps in Montana country. Oh, there was good profit in these pilgrims if a man knew how to handle them.

IV

Comanche John pulled his pony down to a trot as soon as it was obvious there would be no pursuit. From atop a knoll he and his two companions could look back on the circled wagons. Already the men were scattering, hitching mule strings, getting ready to push on across the hill trail to Fort Landen.

"Think they'll ever make it?" Steve asked.

There was worry in his voice. John knew the reason. It was

on account of his girl back there. With the excitement of escape over, he had had time to think about the Sioux. It probably seemed to him that he was abandoning her. The parson apparently felt about the same.

"Shucks," drawled John, "they stood off the Sioux once, they'll do it again. There's been plenty of wagon strings smaller than that one pulled through while the Sioux and Crows was on the prod."

They rode for a couple of hours with John in the lead. They had no destination—they just kept in the general direction of that gap in the mountains where Fort Landen lay. The wagon train dropped out of sight, but when they paused to look back, there would always be a rising haze of dust to give its general location.

John pulled his pony down, and pointed a grimy finger off toward a purplish cluster of mountains to the northwest. "Yonder, beyond them hills a piece, is the Salt River Range. And, after that, the Snake. Then, to the northward, cross some lava plains and you come to the Lemhi. And, after that, the gold camps of the Salmon. I always had a longin' to see them camps." He watched Steve from the corner of his eye. "Gold! That's the stuff. Pretty, and yaller, and easy to carry. She weights down a man's pants good, and makes him feel like somethin'. Gold is different from wheat, or turnips. You can bury her and leave her for a hundred years, and she won't rot. You can throw her in the fire and burn her till doomsday, and then you can pan the ashes, and she'll still be thar. Every color. Like the parson said in one o' his sermons . . . 'Lay up your treasures not in greenbacks which moths and dust do corrupt . . . put her in gold a thousand fine.' You don't want to go farmin', son. Farmin' is for squaws and Chinee. You come with me and we'll go for the yaller gold!"

"By moonlight!" snorted the parson.

"No, Parson, not by moonlight. I admit to stickin' up a coach or three, here and there, and now and then, as the song about me says. But I never asked a young man to jine me. I ain't one to lead youth astray. My conscience wouldn't stand for it. Besides, an inexperienced hand always scrambles the job. How about that there gold, Steve?"

Steve shook his head. "Sorry, John. I think I'll string along in sight of that wagon train. You understand how it is."

"Sure," said John sadly. "Reckon I understand."

He said no more about the gold camps of the Salmon. The three men rode on through the rising country, keeping to the timber that fringed the long ridges, pausing at hill promontories to watch for Indian sign. Behind them a smoke signal strung up through the still, hot air. Perhaps it was marking the position of the train. A second smoke rose in the north half an hour later, then a third, almost out of sight in the far distance.

"Sioux?" asked Steve.

"Or Crow, or Blackfeet, which is just as bad," John answered, watching that distant smoke from beneath the brim of his hat. "You know some ways of lookin' at it, them Injuns is mighty nigh as smart as humans. Look at the Pony Express. Took mighty nigh onto a week to get a message from Fort Hall to Leavenworth. Give a dozen Injuns an armload of green sagebrush apiece, and they'd get her through from dawn to dark."

At twilight they paused by a trickle of cold water and baked stick bread over a little, smokeless fire of aspen twigs. Five or six miles back along the valley they could see the twinkle of camp light where the train had paused for the night.

The hours of darkness passed without the sound of gunfire, so evidently the Sioux had not returned. Morning came, and the three men decided to push on to Fort Landen ahead of the wagon train.

About mid-afternoon, Comanche John wheeled his horse abruptly into the aspen brush that formed a solid wall along the trail. The parson stopped to peer ahead.

"Injuns, ye danged fool," John muttered.

The parson saw them then—a half-dozen warriors, dressed only in breechclouts and moccasins, carrying rifles, bows and arrows, and painted buffalo-hide shields. They were a hundred paces away, just visible through the overhanging brush.

Steve made it down in John's tracks without attracting their notice. The parson tried to urge his horse, but the animal was balky. The parson quirted him. The horse snorted and crashed down through the dry brush.

One of the warriors whooped and wheeled his horse in circles, signaling behind him with upraised thumb. A couple of the others pointed their half-wild ponies toward a small, rocky promontory from which they could look down on the creekbed.

A little, yard-wide stream appeared and disappeared among the bramble. Beyond was a steep bank where fungus-grown basaltic rock poked out.

John splashed his horse up the stream as far as the brush tangle would let him. There was a lot of shouting up the trail, and the *thuds* of galloping horses. He turned and climbed the bank. After twenty or thirty yards, the bottoms opened up a little—a grassy meadow with little bowers of chokeberry and thorn apple.

The Indians were behind somewhere, fanning through the bushes. John turned right, leading the way around some talus rocks that had rolled from the steep hillside. A grassy shoulder of the hill gave them a chance to gallop, but they had no protection there. They were in full view of the Indians back on the trail. One of them drew a bead with his long-barreled flintlock. John snapped a shot from the hip. The ball must have burned the rump of the Indian's pony by the way he lit out, bucking.

Once over that shoulder, the cries of the warriors seemed far away—farther and farther as a mat of spruce timber sponged up the sound. A deer trail led them around the hill, climbing continuously. They came to the edge of the timber and looked down.

The valley was revealed for a considerable distance. Right below, eighty or ninety Sioux were combing the brush, but they were only a part of the total force. There must have been two hundred more strung along up the trail.

"Ge-hosophat!" marveled John, "look at the size of that war party."

A force of two hundred armed warriors was considered an unusually large one. Three hundred on the ground was a few more than John had stomach for.

John noticed that Steve was looking at him. The anguished expression in the young man's eyes made him uncomfortable.

"Think they'll stand a chance?" asked Steve.

"The wagon train? Not if those Injuns get 'em strung out in the valley. They'll come down from two sides at once and cut 'em to pieces."

"Then I'm going back to warn them."

"Me, too!" said the parson. "You better go on to Fort Landen, John. I don't expect your neck would be very safe around that train just yet."

"Neither would yours without me along. I'll take care of myself all right."

There was a sweep of open country to the north of this

wooded hill. The horses took it at a stiff gallop. They swung back to the valley trail several miles east. There were no Indians in sight there. They kept on, gallop and trot, as fast as the horses could take it.

The sun was dipping toward the hills when the wagon train came in sight, creeping along at its turtle's pace. Sells was in the lead, riding his big chestnut horse. Blackfoot was a few paces behind, and Lesh came galloping alongside a few moments later.

"Oh, for a two-pounder cannon and a pocketful of grape," moaned John, looking at those three varmints.

Sells drew rein and watched, his face going ugly from frustration and rage when he recognized who it was. He would probably have gone for his guns if it had only been the parson and Steve, but the presence of Comanche John made him change his mind.

"Well?" he demanded in a harsh voice.

"Why, how-de-do," said John, jolting to a stop and looking at Sells with a sour twist to his lips. "How ye comin' with your knot-tyin' these days?"

Sells let the jibe go, holding his temper. He was wondering why these men had risked their lives by coming back. He waited for some explanation, but none was offered. The parson drew up for a second, then started on impatiently toward the approaching wagons. John, however, stayed where he was.

"Comin'?" shouted the parson.

"Believe I'd rather stay here and let the train catch up. They's some folks I don't fancy turnin' my back on."

Bender was jolting along in the high seat of that first wagon. His jaw was thrust out, and veins were corded on his forehead when he looked down on them. "What the tarnation . . . ?" he started, pulling up the ribbons, giving them a twist around the hand brake. His wife, a tall, drab woman, poked her head through the peep hole and said something, but Bender quieted her with an impatient glance over his shoulder. He never let womenfolk interfere with the way he ran the outfit. "This means hangin', you understand?" he roared at Comanche John. "We won't have you here. None of you. . . ."

"Hold on now, Bender," the parson cackled, shaking his head like an animated scarecrow. "We didn't come back here because we had any hankerin' for your company. We came back here to warn you of an Injun party we run across eight, ten mile up the trail."

Bender placed a foot on the high, front wheel and let himself to the ground, grunting after the manner of big men who are called on to exert themselves too much. He squinted suspiciously into the parson's eyes. "What say?"

"I said there was a war party of Sioux up the trail yonder eight or ten mile, you unwashed idiot! Hundreds of 'em!"

"Hundreds?"

"That's what I said . . . hundreds. There's three hundred if there's a one."

The next wagon had pulled up beside Bender's, filling the trail. Two or three after it came to a stop. Muleskinners walked up wearily in their dusty, patched boots. Sells saw he had an audience, so he shouted his opinion of the parson's tale with a coarse burst of laughter. "Three hundred! Of all the damned lies!"

His tone raised spirits a little. The thought of three hundred armed savages was enough to make a man's guts crawl around like a bundle of snakes, especially when you had a woman and young 'uns back in the wagon. But perhaps, as Sells said, it was only a lie—just another story cooked up by John and the parson to scare them into going south.

Sells went on, jeering: "If you'd made it seventy-five, Parson, maybe some of us would have believed you. But *three hundred!* Why, that's an army. It's more Sioux warriors than you'd find by combin' the country west of Fort Laramie."

"Maybe they ain't Sioux, but they're Indians, and they're primed to take white men's hair, judgin' by the reception they gave us."

"Stick to one story, Parson. Maybe they was Chinooks from over the mountains."

The muleskinners burst into laughter. The parson heard them, and his rage mounted to Old Testament proportions. He rode close to Sells, shaking his bony fist. "Laugh, gol dang ye! But remember this . . . there's women and kids back yonder in them wagons! Women and kids to be run down, and tomahawked, and scalped. You're a man. You ain't got a family. You got a fast hoss. You can light out if this business turns into a massacre, just like you did that time before when. . . ."

There was that accusation again—the one Sells could not endure. He reached out, throttling the parson, twisting his linsey shirt, snapping his old gray head back and forth. Then he stopped abruptly and released him. His eyes had traveled over to Comanche John whose right arm was dangling very loose and whose eyes had become thin and cold as on that day when he had sent a bullet through Alvis Tucker's forehead.

More men were coming up, and Sells shouted to them: "Do you hear the story they've cooked up now? Not *thirty* Injuns, or *fifty* like maybe attacked us the other night. No sir-ee! They come along with three hundred! Why, that's more'n three times as many Injuns as I ever saw in one single war party in all the twelve years I been fightin' 'em."

Sells probably did think it was a lie. The parson turned to the others and wailed: "Listen here, I saw 'em! Have I ever told a lie to you about anything? Have I?"

Sells had an answer for that, too—"You sort of lied when you came out hidin' that pistol under your Bible the other day, Parson."

The parson turned to Bender. "Well, what do you aim to do?"

"Why, go on to Fort Landen, of course."

"I won't let you! I won't allow you to bull head this train right into a massacre. There's women and kids along. . . ."

John said impatiently: "Come on, Parson! You're just wearin' out your lungs."

"Ding blast their hides. . . ."

"Let's git."

"Oh, no you don't!" roared Bender. "We got a score to settle with you, Comanche John. You're a killer, and you got hangin' comin'. . . ."

"Why, so I have."

John hitched his left leg up around the horn of his saddle and looked around at the men on the ground, chewing with considerable amusement. "A course, you ain't exactly got me in irons yet. And maybe I got some objections. Twelve of 'em. The exact number of slugs in my Navies. You know, it might be interestin' at that . . . just to see how many I could get with twelve pistol balls."

"You can't bullyrag this whole train." Bender said it as though he meant it, but neither he nor any of the others made a move for their guns. He looked beyond John at Steve James. "You ought to be ashamed of yourself, Steve. Throwin' in with a road agent. I wonder what your paw would think of you if he was alive today?"

"Those Indians are out there, Bender. I saw them, or I wouldn't have risked my hide coming back."

"Lies! Throw in with road agents, and now lie for 'em. I've

listened to all I'm goin' to. Git out of the trail, all three of you! Hit the timber, because if you're here at camp time, so help me I'll see that all three of you is hung!"

Bender placed a heavy boot on the hub and climbed back to the seat. His old woman, who had listened to all of this, spoke to him: "Paw, I'm scared they're tellin' the truth."

"You go back thar! Get to mixin' your biscuits, that's woman's work. I've brung you this far safe and sound, and I'll get you the rest of the way. I ain't a man that goes around askin' other folks' advice."

Bender's wife pulled her head back inside. He swung his whip across the backs of his eight-mule string. "Git-ap!" he bellowed. "It's ho! for Fort Landen and the green fields of I-dee-ho!"

The parson shouted over the rattle of draw chains and the creak of the wagon: "Recollect the days that the Bible tells about! Recollect the deluge! They laughed at Noah, too, and behold! . . . there was destruction across the face of the earth."

"Go jump in the creek, Noah!" laughed Sells raucously, feeling mighty good over the way it had turned out. "You better get to goin' in your ark before them five hundred Injuns catch up with you."

"Circle those wagons! They'll cut this train up in chunks and. . . ."

"Git-ap!" bellowed Bender.

Bender's string started up the trail, the next wagon fell in, and so on down the line. The parson was forced to draw back and let them roll by. Most of the men were laughing and talking to one another—but a trifle more loudly than was necessary just to keep up their confidence. There was a little suspicion that the parson *might* have been telling the truth. In fact, one skinny man who rode astraddle one of his wheel mules came right out with his suspicions. He growled: "Well, it wouldn't hurt to circle up here and scout around, would it? Just in case?"

"Thar goes your flock, Parson," John said, chewing slowly.

"Just like the children of Israel," the parson moaned. "Following false prophets with a jeer on their lips, never dreamin' of the lightnin' that's about to fall."

"What do you aim to do?"

"Why, stay here and do the best I can."

"How about you, Stevie?"

Steve was watching for Denton's wagon and did not even hear the question.

John gave his leg a disgusted whack. "Then I'll stay, too. But I call it outrageous . . . a man of my reputation, ridin' to doom for the sake of a flock o' pilgrims who tried to hang him and then sneered in his face. I always thought I'd go down to glory, both guns blazin', robbin' a six-horse stagecoach double guarded. . . ."

"Hush up!" The parson was impatient. He kept watching the faces of scared women and kids that looked from the backs of covered wagons. No laughter there about his three hundred Indians!

V

The wagons rolled through some rocky narrows, slowly, their numbers seeming like an elongated serpent. Beyond those narrows, the valley was fairly straight, with hills coming down, forming a gentle V. There were patches of spruce and pine here and there, with yellowish aspen trees growing along the streambed.

Four scouts worked the country up ahead, staying closer than they had out on the prairie. A half hour of this. An hour. The sun was dipping toward the timbered horizon up the valley. There was no breeze. Toward the north a half dozen eagles were flying in steep circles. John, who had been riding near Denton's wagon, pulled up to watch them. The parson stopped, too.

"Carrion, likely," said John. But he saw something else—a patch of serviceberry with tops waving. Waving—but there was no breeze. He spurred forward, and drew up by Bender's wagon. "Injun sign, Bender!"

Bender was tempted to ignore the warning, but something about John's manner told him not to. One of the scouts must have suspected something, for he wheeled and rode back across the hillside. His horse reared, and broke into a frightened run. The scout went over his side, fingers clutching his chest. He had been struck through by an iron-tipped arrow.

"Injuns!" bellowed John.

Bender's wife screamed, and that scream carried more force than anything John could shout. The hillside still seemed deserted for a few seconds—and then, in twenty places, it came to life. Indians appeared from nowhere—from among little clumps of rose thorn, from behind rocks. Several were within stone's throw of the trail and had escaped notice of the scouts. These closest ones sent a hail of bullets and arrows into the wagons. A driver fell from his high seat, frightening his mule string. They snorted, plunging into the rear of the wagon ahead of them, jerkline and straps in a tangle, leaders down with swing team and wheelers trampling over them. They got up and ripped to one side, going through brush down the steep bank of the creek with the wagon careening behind them.

High on the hillside the main body of the Sioux appeared,

riding from a patch of spruce timber. They did not gallop as they would have back on the prairie. The ground was too rough and rock-strewn. They came in a rapid, zigzag trot.

Bender wheeled his lead team, trying to turn the first segment of the train and form some sort of a circle, but this was a prairie tactic. It was impossible to form a circle here with the creek on one side.

Comanche John looked back along the line. The wagons were ramming one another, making a perfect mix-up for the Sioux to butcher them. Cursing all pilgrims, he spurred back, bellowing for drivers to turn their teams toward the creek and in that way to form several tight groups with the stern ends of the Conestogas pointed toward the hillside. Wagons like that could put up a mean fight—especially with the steep creek-bank to be defended on the other side.

A hundred yards of open hillside now separated the charging Indians from the trail. Out of the mêlée of frightened animals and pitching Conestogas came a burst of rifle fire. Here and there a warrior fell from his horse; the rest came on, pushing to a gallop down the rock-strewn slope. Hand brakes were set and drivers jumped to the ground, setting up a devastating criss-cross of bullets.

The fighting became savage, with every man for himself, with no man knowing what the fellow at the next wagon was doing. And, somehow, the Indians were turned back.

Comanche John had been crouched in the protection of a wagon wheel, shooting and reloading until the barrels of his Navies were hot to the touch. He got to his feet and looked around. The sun had dipped beyond the mountains, so that battle had lasted longer than he thought. Three quarters of an hour, perhaps.

Whites and Indians had fallen among the wagons, but the kids had been safe enough behind those high, hardwood planks of the Conestogas, and with furniture and feather ticks stacked around to boot. Nothing like feather ticks to stop rifle ball or arrowhead.

From the hillsides, Indians kept up a steady, long-range popping. Night settled in with none of the usual dinnertime cheer. There were no cook fires, only a dinky mass of coals beneath the overhanging creekbank where the parson kept water boiling for use in his rude surgery.

Finally the desultory gunfire died away. There was silence —a tight, uneasy silence. Minutes would go by. A rifle would send out a streak of flame, starting a rattle around the rocky hillsides, then silence again. The wagoners crouched behind barricades, watching and listening. The moon came up, lighting the country.

John slouched over to find the parson. His fire had become a heap of ash-covered coals, and he was gone. Visiting one of the bereaved families likely.

Up at Bender's wagon he heard Sells say something. Bender answered shortly, his voice gruff. John went back and sat by the wagon wheel. He dozed, and came awake at sound of a new fury of gunfire at the forward end of the train. To the north, the moonlit hillside was filled with movement.

A dozen Indians charged in from nowhere, screaming war cries. John cut loose with his Navies. A muleskinner with a sawed-off shotgun lent a hand. More came—and more. The middle of the train was cut by charging Sioux. A group of muleskinners battled them away—first with bullets, and then with rifles swung like clubs.

Finally the Indians retreated, still shouting, firing guns and arrows from the shadows. Their charge had been turned—but they would be back for more. No one doubted that.

Bender got up, kicking the stiffness from his knees. He

loaded his pistol, thrust it in his belt, and laid the rest of his armaments against the wagon wheel. Then he started down the creek to see how the rest of the people were faring. His wagon formed the keystone of a group of six. After these, there was an opening for fifteen or twenty strides in the middle of which Sells and his two henchmen had built a little barricade of furniture and end gates. At the moment, no one was manning it.

Four or five men were over by McMeels's wagon. Someone was wounded, and, from the fuss he was making, the wound was being probed. He recognized Comanche John's voice, offering advice.

Bender walked along, thinking over the events of the last three weeks. He knew now that Comanche John had been on the square. He knew that the parson had been right in advising the south trail by way of Jim Bridger's, and he knew that he, Bender, had been a stubborn fool, that he had let Sells dupe him and lead him through the worst Indian country in the West just so he could trade a few mules and supplies.

Bender was on his way to look at the wounded man when a sound just beyond the steep cut of the creek made him listen. It was the jingle of bit chains, the stamp of a horse on soft earth. He walked through a low growth of buck brush and looked down. It was shadowy, but he could make out a dark, rangy horse and a man standing beside him, pulling the latigo of a saddle tight.

Bender started down the bank. It was steeper than he expected, and the loose dirt caved with him. He slid to the bottom. Dust rose, blinding him for a second. Then he recognized Sells. He knew what Sells was about. He had lost his guts. Either that, or he had given up hope of ever getting the train through and decided it as just a poor business gamble.

Anyway, he was saddling to try a sneak through the Indian lines. He was doing the exact thing the parson said he would.

Sells whirled around when he heard Bender behind him. "Blackfoot?" he asked.

Then he recognized Bender, crashing toward him through the knee-high brush, drawing his pistol as he came.

"What the devil?" Sells cried.

Bender cursed him. "So you're running out! The parson was right about you all the time. You're a coward like he said. You'd take us through to Fort Landen if it came handy, and run out on us if it didn't!"

"Point that gun some other way."

"It's pointed where it should be. I'm goin' to shoot your guts out, Sells!"

Sells had no doubt that Bender meant what he said. He argued, stalling for time, for a few minutes until Blackfoot or Lesh could come up. "You're wrong, Bender. Listen . . . I can see how it looks, me down here saddling up. But I wasn't running out. I was going to take my life in my hands and sneak through to the fort for help. It's only one night's ride over there if you know all the short cuts. . . ."

"A night's ride! It's a three-day ride!"

"No, Bender, listen. I wasn't running out."

"It's no use, Sells. I'm going to. . . ."

"Bender, don't make a mistake. You'd never forgive yourself if you killed me and then found out the truth. . . ." Sells could see a man approaching along the creek—a big fellow who trod the soft dirt on noiseless moccasins—Blackfoot. Sells raised his voice so Blackfoot would know what was going on: "Bender, don't kill me! Give me half a minute, anyway. My God, at least give me time to pray!"

Blackfoot drew up a dozen steps and slowly lifted the percussion rifle in his hands. Bender couldn't see him. Sells knelt down as though to pray. The rifle roared, smashing Bender forward. He staggered a few steps with his pistol dangling in his hand, and plowed face first into the dirt. The slug had torn his heart.

"What the hell?" asked Blackfoot, coming up and looking at the saddled horse.

"I wasn't going to run out and leave you here," Sells said defensively.

"Oh, no? Then where's my horse?"

"Find your own damned horse. He's over there in the brush. Maybe Lesh is bringin' him."

Blackfoot grunted, lowering his rifle. It was a double, one barrel rifled and one barrel for shot, and he still had the shot for anyone who tried to double-cross him. "Think we can get through them Sioux?" he asked.

"How do I know? We stand a better chance on the run than we do holed up here. This train will be cut to ribbons before the night is over."

Blackfoot turned and started through the bushes for his horse. Sells watched him darkly, but waited.

Over by the wagons, Comanche John had heard Blackfoot's shot and seen the flash it made. A peculiar thing about that flash—it was pointed straight down the wagon train. A man shooting at an Indian would have pointed the other way. He noticed that Sells and his two men were not around. He walked to the edge of the bank.

There he caught sight of Sells, standing beyond his saddled horse. Sells saw him at the same time. Sells would have drawn and fired, but the horse was between them. He didn't care to expose himself by standing high and shooting across the horse's back. So he bent over, keeping the animal between them. "Blackfoot!" he called.

Blackfoot turned. Lesh was coming up from the creek,

leading his horse. They both heard Sells, and then saw John silhouetted there at the crest of the bank.

Lesh went for the pistol at his belt, and Blackfoot started around with his rifle. John's Navies were out. They roared, right and left, with only a fraction of time between them. Blackfoot was hit. He dropped his rifle and crashed away, falling through dry brush. Lesh had leaped aside, and John's second bullet missed.

Lesh went to the ground shoulder first. Lying on his side, he pulled the trigger, aiming at that place on the bank where John had been a second before. But John had slid to the bottom. He remained there, guns drawn and back pressed against the dirt. He was quiet for a few seconds. Then Lesh saw something—or thought he did. He shot. The light that leaped from the muzzle of his gun revealed him momentarily. John squeezed the trigger of his right-hand Navy, and a gunfighter's instinct told him that the bullet had connected.

Sells had been edging around his horse for a shot. The horse became frightened at the shooting and commenced to plunge. Sells tried to keep a grip on the bridle, but he was flung to the ground. His gun was knocked from his fingers. He made a frenzied clutch across the dark earth for them—and then he glimpsed John above him, Navies in his hands. Instantly he sprang from the ground, tangling with John, carrying him back, forcing those two Navies high and out of the way.

Comanche John was strong, but he was no match for Sells. No man in that wagon train, not even the dead Bender himself, would have been a match for Sells in a simple contest of strength. He twisted the Navies from John's grasp. They fell to earth. Sells thrust him on, trying to pin him against the bank. John went suddenly backward with collapsed legs, striking the ground, carrying Sells off balance.

Sells would have landed on him, but John, quick as a bobcat, doubled his legs, and drove his heavy jackboots into Sells's abdomen. The big man was lifted from his feet. He staggered back over his own heels. He struck the dirt bank and fell.

John had no idea of giving him a chance to rise. There could be none of your polite formalities about this fight. It was to be to the finish, and no quarter given. John charged, intending to swing his jackboots to Sells's head.

Sells was sick from the blow he had taken, but he still had strength left to get up and clamber the bank. John followed. Sells ran toward the barricade, looking for a weapon. His bullwhip was there, coiled where he had left it. He snatched it up and set himself. Its long lash snaked out, aimed for John's eyes, but John fended it off with his forearm. He retreated, looking from side to side for a weapon—any weapon. A rifle was leaning against a wagon wheel, where someone had left it, and up above, in its socket by the high seat, was a whip.

Sells came to a stop, thinking John was going for that rifle. Instead, John came around holding the whip. He swung out its heavy leather lash with a practiced swing, and drew back with a powerful twist of back and shoulder muscles so that it echoed like a pistol. John spoke: "You've been mighty fancy with that whip o' yourn. Might-ee fancy. But I've skinned a few mules myself. So I have a hankerin' to find out if you north-country 'skinners have added anythin' to the art."

Sells laughed. This was a contest he would enjoy. He advanced and swung his whip like a striking rattlesnake. But in a test of quickness Comanche John was top dog. He spun to one side, feeling the burn against his cheek bone as the popper tore a fragment from the brim of his black slouch hat. While Sells's lash was still straight out, John swung his whip.

Sells saw it coming. He thought it was aimed for his head.

He bent double to avoid it. Instead, the lash wrapped in sudden coils around his pivot foot. John wheeled, spilling Sells backward. "That's the old Sacramento twist!" he yipped. "Now I'll show ye one I learnt in Ten-Spot Gulch!"

Sells struggled to his feet while the next cut of John's whip tore a fragment from his buckskin shirt. He set himself swinging with every ounce of his magnificent bulk, aiming at John's throat.

It was a killing blow. If it landed right, it could tear the jugular to pieces. But John moved the few inches that were necessary and the whip cracked past his ear. He balanced a bare fraction of a second, and then swung, guessing Sells's follow-up movement. The long lash flew out to Sells, wrapping around his neck.

John dug in his heels and pulled back. Sells went down. He dropped his whip and tore at the leather coils with both hands. He got free somehow, and rolled away, gasping for breath.

Indians were whooping out there in the moonlight, charging the wagon train. Sells didn't seem to notice. He was terrified by that whip. A flaming arrow started a roll of fire in the top of a Conestoga, casting light on him as he ran toward the hillside. He suddenly seemed to realize that he was only running from one death into another. He turned and started back. A tall Sioux warrior was right behind him.

The warrior had fired his rifle. He flung it away and slid a short bow from his naked shoulder. Fast as an eye wink, his hand came up from his quiver, fitting an arrow in the bow sinew. His arm swung back with the power of shoulder and back behind it, driving the arrow so its four-inch iron head smashed bone and flesh, passing completely through Sells's chest and rattling among the spokes of a wagon wheel beyond. Sells still ran, his legs working automatically, although death had touched his eyes. He slumped forward and lay still.

Scarcely anybody noticed him, not even Comanche John. He dropped his whip, leaped over to the bank to retrieve his Navies, and came charging back to open up on the Sioux.

Women carried water from the creek to drench the wagons. They swung wet quilts to beat out flames. Their men fought the Sioux back with bullets, and with the stocks of their rifles when the battle became close.

At dawn there was silence. The Indians had long retreated and, at last, could be seen riding a ridge to the west.

That night, under the command of Cy Denton, the train wheeled back for the prairie. They struck the old north-south trapper's trail along the eastern edge of hill country and followed it southward in the direction of Bridger's fort.

On the fourth day they reached the deep ruts of the Oregon Trail. Then it was that Comanche John dumped a week's provisions in his saddlebags and squinted off toward the south. "I hear plenty talk about gold comin' in big, yaller hen's eggs from gravel down Pike's Peak way," he said. "Better come along and git some, Parson."

The parson shook his head. "No, John. Reckon I'm still needed here."

"Shucks, a locoed hoss with blinders on could find the trail to I-dee-ho, and you've preached a sufficiency of funerals to last you for a while, I reckon."

"I've preached a heap too many funerals." The parson pointed at the high seat of a wagon where Steve James and Mary Denton were riding. "Thing I look forward to preachin' is a weddin'."

Smoke Talk

It was the stormy end of November, a treacherous month in Montana Territory, and, by the time Comanche John rode up to the stage station, a howling wind was sweeping from the direction of Canada. The Reverend Jeremiah Parker, skinny and old, creaked outside and tossed a leg over his pinto horse.

"I dare say it was quite a sacrifice, tearing yourself free of that Diamond City stud game," he said in his querulous, magpie voice.

"Stud game! Why, Parson that's slander." Comanche John shot tobacco juice into the November gale and grinned through his tangle of black whiskers. "You know my opinion o' cyards. Cyards are an invention of the devil. Steppin' stones to Denver, and anybody knows that Denver is right next door to hell. Cyards are the devil's prayer book o' fifty-two pages, fifty-three countin' the joker."

The parson made an exasperated gesture, bending forward with head lowered against the wind. John didn't seem to mind the weather. He rode slouched and careless as always, a broad figure in black hat, beaded Cree jacket, gray homespun trousers stuffed in the tops of horsehide jackboots. Around his waist, hitched a little for comfort in riding, were two Navy Colts.

"I was late," Comanche John said righteously, "because I took the time to solicit an offering for a religious charity. To wit . . . that mission you hanker to build over at Bullion Bar."

"How much?" asked the parson.

"Considerable," drawled Comanche John.

News of the offering mollified the parson, for the Bullion

Bar mission was one of his most cherished ambitions. They rode into the wind as night settled. It had been snowing a little all day, and now the air became choked with slanting white flakes. A gulch guided them through unknown, bare-sided hills. Unexpectedly from the storm whirl they caught sight of a lighted cabin window.

"That's the advantage o' havin' a preacher along," said John, reaching a jackboot for the ground. "You know that Providence is on your side."

He waded eight inches of snow and rapped at the rude, whipsawed panels of the door. When there was no answer, he exerted a little pressure. The door was barred on the inside.

"Hey in thar!" he roared. "This is no way to treat poor, frozen Christians in a storm!"

Finally a voice answered—a woman's voice. "Who is it?" she asked.

"It's me!" Comanche John started to tell his name and thought better of it. "Tell her who we be, Parson."

"I'm the Reverend Jeremiah Parker, and the man with me is John Smith. We were headed for Bullion Bar when the storm caught us."

After a considerable wait there was a thumping sound of a bar being removed, and the door opened. A slender, dark-haired girl was backing toward the far wall, an aimed rifle in her hands.

John lifted his hands. "Ma'am, don't get that finger to itchin'. We come in here as peaceful as two jack rabbits at a rattlesnake's convention. The parson, yonder, don't even carry a gun, and I wouldn't neither if they didn't balance my walk."

"I'm just a humble servant of the Lord!" chimed the parson.

The girl slowly lowered the rifle. "I'm sorry," she said.

"I'm really awfully sorry. You understand how it is when a woman's all alone."

"You live way out here *alone?*" gasped John.

She nodded her head, and there was something resembling defiance in her eyes. She took time to rebar the door.

Comanche John warmed his hands at the cook stove. He noticed a pipe with a half-burned bowl of tobacco on the rough-board table. When the girl looked away, he touched the pipe. The bowl was still warm, and a faint odor of tobacco still hung in the air.

She turned and saw him take his hand away. "Why did you do that?" she asked in an edgy voice.

John calmly chewed his tobacco, taking his time about answering. "I was just a mite surprised to see a pretty young gal smokin' a pipe."

His tone seemed to reassure her. She smiled a little, although her young face was still worried and rather pale. "Lots of women smoke pipes."

John sat down on a bench and met her eyes. "What's wrong here, anyhow?" he demanded.

"Nothing!"

John shrugged. He unbuttoned his beaded jacket, and stretched out his jackboots. A few drops of snow melted from them, making tiny, clear puddles on the scrubbed, split-pole floor.

"Minin' claim here?" he asked.

She nodded. Suddenly she leaped forward to stand, rigid and listening, by the door. After a few seconds they could hear the jingle of bridle chains and the squeaky, crunching sounds that horses make in new snow. She grabbed up the rifle, but Comanche John's hand closed on the barrel.

"I'll take it, gal."

"No!" She clenched her teeth, breathing hard through her

thin nostrils, trying to wrench it away.

John took it from her and leaned it against the wall. "Reckon I can take care o' any unpleasantness," he grinned through his tangled black whiskers. "I'll harry 'em and the parson will bury 'em."

The man rattled the door. "Bud Atterly, we know you're in thar! Do you come out peaceful, or do we have to smoke you out?"

"Better open it," said John.

The girl lifted the bar. A hulking, heavy-shouldered man filled the opening. He blinked snowflakes from his eyelashes and scanned the room over the girl's shoulder.

"What's come over you, Doyle?" she demanded. "Put up that Colt pistol when you come inside my house!"

Doyle stalked past her, the gun still in his hand. He turned on her then, taking time to rub some icicles off his droopy red mustache. "This ain't no friendly visit, Gail. I'm here as a leader of a posse. This is the law!"

"Vigilante law!"

"It's all the law there is in this territory, I reckon." He looked suspiciously at Comanche John and the parson. "I never seen these men before."

"They're friends of mine."

Doyle grunted something and strode through the house, leaving a trail of melted snow behind him. Half a dozen men had followed him inside by that time. One, a skinny, hawk-faced man with predatory eyes and two guns in tied-down holsters, elbowed his way forward and stood facing the girl.

"You might as well tell where your brother's hid out."

"Why should I? He hasn't done anything."

"He robbed my bank! Robbed it of eight thousand dollars in greenbacks. . . ."

"That's a lie!" The girl was trembling a little. "We've taken considerable dirt off you in the last couple of years, and it's about time we. . . ."

"Now, Gail," Doyle temporized, rubbing his droopy mustache. "Such talk ain't goin' to do a bit of good. Mister Roose didn't mean to. . . ."

"*Mister* Roose! You're like everybody else. As soon as he gets money, you're willing to forget that he's only a dry-gulching killer."

Roose smiled unpleasantly, showing his teeth between tightly drawn lips. "I already know what you think of me, but that doesn't alter the fact that your brother robbed my bank."

"He couldn't have. He was right here at noon. He'd have needed a relay of horses."

"Then he had 'em."

Doyle said: "It's no use arguin', Gail. We picked up his trail in the snow and followed it here. Besides that, your brother was identified."

"Who identified him?"

"Waal, there was Pike Hixon, yonder. He ought to remember pretty good, because he's packin' a slug from one of Bud's guns in his shoulder right this minute. Ask Pike who it was shot him when he came out o' the bank."

Pike Hixon was short, burly, and ill-tempered. He carried his left arm in a sling improvised from a black neckerchief. He'd opened his long, rat-skin fur coat to absorb some heat from the fire, revealing a marshal's badge. Hixon growled: "Hell, Doyle, what's the use of all this talk? We all know it was Atterly, so the quicker we fit him with a rope cravat, the better."

"Of course, you know it was Bud," the girl cried, spinning on him. "*You'd* know! Everyone in this room knows you're Simon Roose's marshal. You're his hired gun hand that took up the marshal job as a sideline."

The girl stood, stiff and suddenly pale. Men were trampling in the back way. Three roughly garbed vigilantes came in, their guns drawn, prodding a tall young man ahead of them. He was a year or two older than the girl to whom he bore a strong resemblance.

"Caught him sneakin' belly down through an old placer trench," one of the vigilantes said. "Made a run for it, but we caught him in a drift. He had his gun out, but Walker fetched him from behind."

Blood was sponging through the young fellow's corn-colored hair, showing where Walker had "fetched" him—probably from behind with the barrel of a rifle.

Roose saw the blood and chuckled, rubbing his palms over the twin butts of his tied-down pistols. "Did you search him for my money?" he asked.

Doyle went over him carefully, finding nothing except a short-bladed hunting knife, a silver watch, and some small change.

Bud Atterly turned on Roose and said: "I haven't been inside that brick-faced swindle you call a bank since you cheated us on that eight thousand dollar note."

There was a second of silence while the men moved uncomfortably, and the November blizzard moaned in the slab-rock chimney.

"Young man, this should teach you a lesson!" Everyone started at the unexpected voice. Comanche John roosted nonchalantly on the edge of the wood box, chewing tobacco and swinging one horsehide jackboot. There was nothing particularly conspicuous about his Navy Colts, but they were hanging against his thighs, butts out, ready. "Any man that robs banks without a mask over his face is just requestin' a hang rope."

"Who are you?" Roose snarled.

"Me? I'm just a buzzard that flew in with the storm."

"What's your name?" Doyle asked.

"Smith. John Smith."

"Whar you from?"

"Bannack."

Roose twisted down the corners of his mouth and stood with hands resting on the butts of his sixes. "Then you better head back for Bannack and keep your nose out of our affairs."

"Hmm!" Comanche John bent over to spurt tobacco juice in the ash hopper. His face, what could be seen of it beyond the tangle of black whiskers, was placid, but his eyes were hard as matched pieces of quartz. "Now that's a thought. Mebby I will, mebby I won't."

"Listen, stranger. . . ."

"Now, ca'm down. I only said that the lad was downright foolish to stick up a bank without a mask in front of his face."

"He *did* wear a mask," growled Hixon.

"He did! Then how in thunder could you identify him?"

"There's lot of things besides a man's face that identifies him."

"Yep," said John placidly. "There shore is. But you must admit that a face is far and away the best."

"Anyhow, we picked up his trail and followed it here."

"Through this blizzard?"

"We followed it to within five miles, and that was close enough."

"Close enough for hangin'?"

"We don't need tintypes showin' him in the act!"

The young man started to talk, his voice high and tightly drawn. "I'll admit I was in Diamond City today, but I didn't rob the bank. I wasn't even near the bank."

Roose cackled. "How about your story that you were here at this cabin at noon?"

"Maybe Sis was trying to make it easier for me. I wasn't here at noon. I was in Diamond City. I went in to see Long Tom Philips."

"You have big business to conduct with millionaire minin' men, I suppose!" Roose sneered.

"I wanted to borrow money to pay off that note of ours that you're holding."

"And what did Long Tom say?"

"He wasn't home."

"And when you found out he wasn't home, you decided you'd put a mask over your face and pay me a nice, friendly call."

"No. I started over to Blakeslee's store for a tin of tobacco. I heard shootin', and pretty soon some strange kids came running down the road saying Bud Atterly had robbed the bank. I knew it would mean a hang rope if I went around to argue that it wasn't me. I knew it was a frame. I just lit out for the ranch."

Roose laughed and said: "Atterly, I'd've thought you'd been able to think up a better story than that."

Bud Atterly was standing by the table. The lamp was quite close. No one realized what he was about when he leaned over. He blew down the chimney, and suddenly the room was dark.

There followed a roar of curses and stamp of heavy boots. Men rammed each other and batted furniture over. Doyle's voice could be heard over everything.

"Stop whar you are, everybody. First man that opens a door gets a bullet in his innards!"

"He got out the back way!" somebody said.

The words almost started a stampede, but Comanche

John's calm drawl stopped it. "Nope, he didn't get out the back way. He's right here."

Doyle opened the front of the stove, lighting the room from blaze of the fire. Comanche John had Bud with arms pinned behind his back. "Take it peaceful, lad, and I'll let you loose."

Bud said something through tight lips. John released him, and with an unexpected twisting movement he went to the floor.

He bounded to a crouch and was trying to weave his way to the door. One of the vigilantes tripped him. He sprawled face foremost. For the moment he was helpless, lying sharply revealed in light from the open door of the stove.

Roose stepped back. His right hand whisked up, dragging a heavy Colt from its tied-down holster.

The parson started forward, but he was too far distant. Bud sensed the gun pointed toward him and staggered to his feet. The room was split by powder flame and explosion, but the lead slug zinged harmlessly through the poles and dirt roof. Comanche John had booted the gun up with a swing of a thick-soled jackboot.

Roose came around with the gun, pain twisting his face. For the moment he was unable to locate his target. Comanche John had backed away, one of the Navy Colts in his hand. "Don't try it, Roose," he warned.

Roose stood, spitting vile words through tight lips. He could see the gun barrel angling his way, and, with a movement so slow John could not misinterpret it, he returned his Colt to its holster. At almost the identical moment, John slid his own gun away.

Roose turned and snarled at Doyle: "Well, what are you waiting for? That should make both of them candidates for a hang rope. . . ."

"Don't forget, I stopped him from gettin' away," John drawled.

"That's right, Roose," Doyle agreed. "He'd likely have got plumb away in the dark if it hadn't been for the Bannack stranger."

The girl sobbed: "Why did you do it?"

"Waal, I wouldn't have except for one thing. I know vigilantes from a long way back, havin' been associated with 'em one way or another down in Californy, and they're mighty hard to get off your trail. And the *one thing* happens to be important."

"What is it?"

"Just that he ain't guilty, and I can prove it."

A couple of men laughed, but John went on serenely chewing his tobacco.

"Yep, I'm willing to forget all about the marshal's identification right through a black mask. I'm even willing to forget that you never found the money, and that, even if he had taken it, it was only what already belonged to him. But by the way, did the bank teller identify him?"

Roose grunted: "Ed Finch was too scared to identify anybody."

"Hmm! Then the only word you're goin' by is Hixon's, here, and it seems like everybody agrees he's nothin' much except the banker's gun-handy."

Hixon came over and stood with feet spread, his left arm still in a sling, his jaw thrust forward aggressively. "Are you trying to say I'm a liar?"

"Waal, no. I'd rather put it this way . . . you're maybe a trifle anxious to agree with your boss."

Hixon started to bellow, but Doyle cut him off. "Let the stranger have his say."

"Why, thank-ee, Doyle. That's uncommon nice, comin'

from a vigilante. Now here's my point . . . if I was a road agent . . ."—Comanche John chuckled as though the idea were far-fetched—"*if* I was a road agent, I'd sure enough take some o' the money with me, if I lit out for the faraway timber like Bud just tried to do. But recollect he had only a dollar or two. . . ."

"Oh, hell," grumbled Hixon. "This fool will jabber all night. Let's hang our road agent and get back to town. I got a slug in my shoulder, and it's hurting me."

"Same slug the road agent handed you when he came from the bank?"

"Yes. He got me in the shoulder. Otherwise I'd have killed him and this trip wouldn't have been necessary."

"Nice shootin'," marveled John. "Didn't you say he'd already shot away your right-hand gun without givin' you a scratch?"

"I don't remember saying so, but he did."

"Yes, sir, that was lovely shootin'. Any of you lads know Bud Atterly was that kind of a gun whanger?"

A posseman laughed: "I can outshoot Bud Atterly any day of his life."

"By the way, let's see that six-shooter you took away from him when you caught him down the gulch."

John examined it. "No empties. Thirty-Eight caliber." He looked at Hixon. "By the way, Marshal, I don't like the idee o' you walkin' around with that slug lodged in your shoulder. You'll be lucky if ptomaine lead poisonin' don't set in before you get to town."

Hixon uttered a hollow laugh, but he ran an apprehensive hand across his wounded shoulder.

John went on. "However, you're plumb fortunate because it just happens that the parson, yonder, is one o' the best free-style probers that ever rode down the rutty road from

Independence in a square-wheeled wagon. How would you like to spread yourself on yonder table while he digs out the slug and slaps on a soap and sorghum poultice?"

The parson fetched a saddlebag and drew out an assortment of probes, scalpels, and bandage that quieted all doubts of his proficiency. The marshal stripped off his shirt and unwound a length of dirty bandage to reveal the wound.

The bullet was not lodged deeply, so it was a short task to extract it. The parson dropped it in the waiting hand of Comanche John.

"Nice condition," John mused. "Just about the way she come out o' the gun bar'l. That's lucky for you, Marshal. Them things ruin a man when they mash up. And I'd say this bullet was lucky for Bud, too."

Everyone was listening now. Comanche John stood with his jackboots spread wide, grinning through tangled black whiskers. With a confident movement, he picked up Bud's .38 and tried to fit the ball in its barrel. It would not have slid in easily even had it not been knocked a trifle lopsided in passing through several inches of the marshal's flesh. "You see? This ball never came from Bud's gun. This is no Thirty-Eight. More like this is a Forty-Four, or maybe even a Forty-Five. Look at it yourselves."

Roose cursed, whirled back toward the door. "He's guilty, damn you! He could have changed guns. You heard Hixon say he was the one. . . ."

"Anybody can be mistaken," said Doyle.

"Damn you, he'll either stretch rope or stop lead. . . ."

Roose's hands came up, weighted with the twin guns from his holsters. Comanche John had weaved back a little. There was no sharp movement, only an easy hitching movement of his shoulders, but the Navy Colts were in his hands, and the room ripped with concussion. Roose was hammered to the wall. He went down, the guns clattering from his hands.

In ten or fifteen minutes the vigilantes left, taking the wounded Roose with them. The cabin seemed roomy and silent without them. The girl brewed coffee, and Comanche John sat on the bench, chuckling with satisfaction.

Unexpectedly the magpie voice of the parson sawed across the room. "John, that was mighty fine shooting outside the bank. Whar's the money?"

John got to his feet. "Now hold on, Parson. That evidence is most circumstantial. . . ."

"Whar's that money you took from the Diamond City bank this afternoon?"

Comanche John chewed and then with a vast sigh spat in the ash hopper. Then he walked outside, returning a couple of minutes later with a Cree-made saddlebag stuffed with greenbacks.

"After all I've done for you," moaned the parson. "After all the months I spent makin' a decent Christian out of you."

"I just lifted it so's I could build you that mission over in Bullion Bar."

"Robbery is robbery."

"Yes, robbery is robbery," said the girl. "Roose robbed us of this much money, but he did it with the fine print in a note we didn't read carefully enough. And now he's going to take this claim away from us. I admire a robber like John a whole lot more."

The parson was thoughtful. "If what you say is true, and I reckon it is, then this money really belongs to you and your brother. Yep, gather it up, my children!"

Squaw Guns

I

He was a trifle under average height—slouched and powerful. He sat with his chair tilted against the rear wall of the log saloon, his dusty hat brim shading his eyes, his face almost concealed by a tangle of black whiskers. From time to time he leaned over to shoot tobacco juice at a knothole in the rough floor, but always his eyes were alert, watching the door and the crowd that passed along the twilit street of Diamond Gulch, Montana Territory.

He was not a Pike's Peaker—not one of those Missouri farmers who started for free land at the end of the Oregon Trail and turned north at news of Idaho and Montana gold. His skin, burned brown as Piegan moccasin, indicated years of Western sun and wind. He wore a fringed buckskin shirt fastened by thongs in place of buttons. Trousers of gray homespun were stuffed in dusty jackboots. Around his waist, sagging from crossed belts, were two Navy Colts.

The evening crowd of prospectors, bullwhackers, and get-rich-quickers were dumping gold and greenbacks on the rough pine bar in exchange for tin cups of raw trade whisky. The whiskered man seemed oblivious to the whooping crowd. He placidly chewed tobacco, sometimes appearing almost asleep, but whenever a man entered from the street, his eyes became gray slits of suspicion.

A tall, closely shaved man came in carrying a Mormon candle in a brass stick, and hung it on a peg near the faro spread. He laid out a brace of Derringers, undraped the box and chips, and drew on black sleeve protectors. Then he announced with a ringing Harvard precision: "Here's what you came from Pike County to find, gentlemen. Easy gold. And you don't even need to wet your feet digging it. Don't trample, gentlemen, there are chips enough for one and all."

Light from the Mormon candle appeared to be a little too bright for the whiskered man's fancy, so he moved his chair. He had just tilted it once more against the wall when someone entered that attracted his special attention. The newcomer was a man of about thirty-five. He was over six feet, the breadth of his shoulders accentuated by his well-cut waistcoat of English kerseymere. His eyes came to rest on the whiskered man. He smiled a little, showing the tips of his perfect teeth. He walked across, hooked a chair with a polished boot toe, drew it over to an unused poker table, and sat down. Then, instead of speaking directly to the whiskered one, he twisted his lips in a whimsical manner and sang.

Comanche John rode to I-dee-ho
In the year of 'Sixty-Two
With a pal named Whisky Anderson
And one named Henry Drew.

The whiskered man answered: "This is Montana Territory, Mecklin, and Henry Drew is dead. Vigilante got him in Bannack, so I hear, and presented him with a necktie as a token o' their esteem. As for Comanche John . . . why, I hear tell he quit robbin' and reformed. Got religion and took to singin' psalms."

Field Mecklin laughed. A little jerk of his head, a flash of perfect teeth, then eyes pale and intent as ever. "I'm not here representing any band of Bannack stranglers, John."

"I didn't reckon you were," Comanche John drawled. "You always been a man that handled his own business in his own way, like me. Reckoned maybe that's why you came in here three deep." He jerked his head at the three gun-toters who had followed Mecklin inside and were now ranged at points of vantage around the room.

One of the men was especially noticeable. He was a huge, greasy-looking man with stringy black hair and thick, overhanging eyebrows, his face drawn out of shape by an old tomahawk wound that had cut deeply in his left cheek bone and ran down to his jaw.

John said: "There's Blackie Andros. Good old Blackie! The man that was coach robber with a gang in the Sierras and sold out his best friend for a poke of vigilante gold. Thanks for bringin' him, because if this here tatey-tate o' ourn gets around to shootin', I don't know of a man I'd rather use for a target."

"There'll be no shooting," Field Mecklin said easily. He rested elbows on the green-topped table, pressing the ends of his finely formed fingers together. "If I wanted to get rid of you, there'd be easier ways. For example, I could tell Buffalo Browers, and I think he'd have his vigilance committee around here in polka time."

Comanche John made no comment. What the man said was true, of course. Field Mecklin was partner in the firm of Enfield & Mecklin that operated stagecoaches between Fort Benton and Salt Lake City, and as head of such a stagecoach empire it was improbable that he would deliberately expose himself to a pair of guns as notoriously swift and deadly as Comanche John's, not even with Blackie Andros and those other two to back him up.

"Drink?" asked Field Mecklin.

Comanche John let his chair thump forward. He dragged

it across the slivery floor and sat with one elbow on the table. Mecklin signaled to the bartender who paid not the least attention.

John bellowed: "Whisky, damn-ee! Whisky before I part your hair with a Forty-Four caliber comb!"

The bartender was a stoop-shouldered man in a reeking, flour-sack apron with a holstered cap-and-ball pistol strapped ponderously around it. He walked to the end of the bar and observed John truculently.

John went on. "And none o' your heathen Blackfoot pizen neither. This yere's a stagecoach king, and he craves the best."

The bartender hooked a jug of trade whisky by the handle and hoisted it to his forearm—reaching for a brace of tin cups.

"Not that bottle." John indicated a fat-bellied quart of Maryland rye that sat on the back-bar for purely decorative purposes. "*That* bottle!"

"What bottle?"

Comanche John's right shoulder barely hitched. There was a heavy concussion. The smoking muzzle of a six-shooter was visible above the edge of the table, and the bottle of Maryland rye stood on the back-bar, its neck neatly severed.

"That one," said John calmly.

The gunshot created scarcely a ripple in the saloon. Some of the customers did not cease talking or glance around. The bartender took down his precious bottle and carried it over.

John blew smoke from the pistol barrel, took a patent brass powder horn from his pocket, reloaded the empty cylinder, and inserted a cap. "I dare say," he drawled, sliding the Navy Colt back, "that you had a piece o' business on your mind when you came huntin' me out."

Mecklin nodded. "Do you have a gang out in the hills?"

"I told ye, Mecklin, I've ree-formed. Seen the errors of my ways. Robbery is a defiance o' the Bible. It ain't ethical in the moral sense. It gets a man to travelin' with bad companions, and it's dee-structive to the health o' the human body, what with the buckshot they've got these days. Why, I even heered that the new legislature down in Virginny City was talkin' about passin' a law ag'in' robbery of all kinds. Mecklin, if you're skeered on account of the gold your coaches are carryin' from this camp, just unhalter your cravat and breathe easy."

Mecklin barely smiled and said: "I know of a coach coming in with fifteen thousand in its strongbox."

Comanche John chewed for a while. He turned to shoot tobacco juice at his favorite knothole. "Why, that's mighty interestin'. Yep . . . might-ee interestin'. Fifteen thousand is a heap o' money. Think of all the good a man could do with fifteen thousand. Think o' churches he could build, the hymn books he could buy. By the way, just what coach has all that gold heaped on her?" John's eyes narrowed.

"It's not gold, it's greenbacks."

"*Them* things! They won't be worth more than five cents on the hundred when Lee takes Noo York."

"Perhaps the greenback has depreciated, but that fifteen thousand would still be worth seven or eight in gold, so it ought to be worthwhile."

There was a Bowie-knife edge to John's voice when he asked: "Just what's your game, Mecklin?"

"What do you care as long as you get the money?"

John's eyes shifted across the room. Blackie Andros stood by the wall at one side of the faro spread, thumbs hooked in gun belts, the scar gash shadowed by candle flame seeming to cut his brutal, greasy face in half. The other two gunmen were pretending to watch a poker game. One of them, a raw-boned man with thin, reddish hair called Baldy, he remembered from Yellow Jacket. He'd ramrodded a crooked card house there. The other was a stranger, although his type was familiar enough—he was one of those sure of being on the strong side when he signs up.

If John had any idea of refusing Mecklin's proposition, knowledge of the bushwhack bullets that might come from the guns of those three deterred him. He said: "I don't give a damn about anything as long as I get the fifteen thousand, Mecklin."

"That's what I thought."

Mecklin poured drinks from the decapitated bottle and spoke in clipped sentences: "It's our Fort Benton coach. The one coming down. Due here tomorrow at dawn. We've instructed the driver to take the lower road through the Belts. There are four miles of narrow going along Longknife Cañon. A couple of deep fords where passengers may have to get out and push. It shouldn't be too much trouble for an old hand like you. The money will be in the strongbox. A word of warning . . . the driver and guard know nothing about it. You'll have to take your own chances. How many men will you have?"

John freshened his chew. "I can't kee-rectly say, Mecklin, thar might be just me . . . me and my two pistols, which o' course, makes three of us. And again thar might be as many as ten o' my boys up in the scrub pine."

Mecklin stood up. "I can figure on it, then?"

"With fifteen thousand in greenbacks waitin', you sure can!"

II

Comanche John watched Mecklin stride through the door with his gunmen following. He stood up and hitched his belts.

"Waal, I'm damned! Fifteen thousand, and the owner of the stagecoach comes around beggin' me to lift it."

He went outside, still mulling the thing over. His talk about ten of his boys was pure fiction, of course. Since parting with Whisky Anderson down on the Beaverhead, he'd played a lone hand, most of the time following the path of rectitude through the good influence of his best friend, the Reverend Jeremiah Parker, known affectionately from the Oregon Trail to Canada as the parson.

The gold camp of Diamond Gulch sprawled along the gulch wherever placer workings would let it. Above and below, he could see elevated flumes and the growing hills of washed gravel dumped from the sluice tails. Along one gutter of the winding street flowed a stream of milky water. A couple of jerk-line ox teams with Conestoga wagons in tandem blocked the street before the W & I Mercantile; from Honey Blanche's place came music of a piano being banged in jig time. A stream of moccasined and booted men passed along the pole sidewalks, and Comanche John fell in with them.

A log building with an unfinished roof stood thirty or forty paces uphill from the main drag. It was surrounded by a rude steeple. Candlelight came through oiled-paper windows. John opened the whipsawed plank door and went inside. A skinny, gray-haired man was pegging legs in a flattened log to turn it into a bench. He peered with a pair of Old Testament eyes. "Oh, thar ye be!"

"Yep, Parson, hyar I be." John recognized his expression and made an exasperated gesture. "Quit lookin' at me thataway. I ain't kilt a man in more'n an hour."

"Killin's nothin' to joke about!" squawked the parson in his parrot voice.

"I told ye I'd reformed, and reformed I be. Seein' all this Diamond Gulch gold ain't changed me a bit." John had been reforming off and on for the better part of two years now, ever since his first meeting with the Reverend Jeremiah Parker near Fort Hall on the Oregon Trail. They had met near Bannack four weeks ago, and the parson had talked him into journeying to Diamond Gulch for "a fresh start"—a suggestion that Comanche John had favored, at least partially because the Bannack Vigilance Committee happened to be on his trail.

John sat down and nudged at a heap of religious tracts with the toe of one jackboot. "Parson, as a man o' the Lord, what's your opinion of a certain high-talkin' gent by the handle of Field Mecklin?"

"Of Enfield and Mecklin?"

"The same."

"A fine gentleman! A fine, God-fearing gentleman! One of the men who will build this great Western land of ours from a howling wilderness to. . . ."

"Then you think any job Mister Mecklin offered me would be honorable as is fitten a bleached sheep like myself."

"You ain't thinkin' of gettin' a job!"

"Parson, I don't exactly cotton to the tone of that reemark. Not that workin' for Mecklin wouldn't lead me from the narrow trail of rectitude."

"What sort of a job?"

"Its nature," said John, "is so ding-blasted confidential that I don't dare breathe a whisper of it to nobody."

★ ★ ★ ★ ★

Comanche John left by the rear door of the parson's half-completed mission and slouched up a rocky pathway to a pole corral at the edge of jack spruce timber. He waited at the gate of this open-air livery for the Mexican proprietor to catch Patches, his wiry little Nez Percé pony.

He mounted and headed down the Last Chance road until the camp disappeared around a bend, then he plunged uphill through quaking asp and serviceberry, following a gully that cut deeply into the mountainside.

It was dark, and he could see the candlelight of Diamond Gulch, the reddish flame of torches lighting placer mines above and below town where sluices worked on a twenty-four hour schedule, tearing coarse gold from the bedrock, rushing to harvest a treasure that had been hoarded by the mountains through a million years.

Diamond Gulch disappeared around the swelling chest of the mountain. He followed a deer trail slanting to a gulch black with spruce. There was a small, transparent stream, a road beyond—the deeply rutted Fort Benton road. He followed the ruts to the foot of Longknife Cañon. There he hid his horse in timber and went on afoot.

It was a narrow cañon. The crooked road crossed and re-crossed the stream. It was after midnight when he sighted Frenchy's station where horses were changed for the last lap to Diamond Gulch. There was a cabin, some pole corrals, a sod-roofed shed. A gaunt dog barked at him. He hammered on the door, and after a time someone moved inside. The door squeaked open a few inches. He was looking into the twin barrels of a sawed-off shotgun.

"I was throwed off my hoss," John said sadly, "and I figured maybe I could borrow one here."

The gun remained steady. "Who is thees?"—the man

asked in a strong Coyote-French accent.

"I'm Jones. John Jones. You know me, Frenchy. I got a claim yonder in Soapstone Gulch."

"Ah!" Frenchy put down the gun. "Come in, *m'shu!*" He lifted the top of the sheet-metal stove and blew on the coals until they brightened enough to light his bear-grease lamp. "Forgive me those gun, *m'shu,* but weeth all thees story about Comanche John I am what you call it? . . . nervass. Ha!"

The lamp made a smoky yellow light in the crude cabin. Frenchy was a medium-statured half-breed, fully dressed in buckskin despite the fact that he had just risen from his spruce-branch bunk.

John said: "You don't need to be scairt o' that varmint, Comanche John. I hear tell he got religion and had to quit chewin' tobacco on account of his mouth bein' so full of Scripture. How about lendin' me that hoss?"

French gestured in sorrow. "All these cayuse in corral, she's coach horse of *compagnie.* If I len' one . . . my job *phouf! Sacré* damn. She's far walk to Soapstone, hey?"

"I'm goin' to town."

"But of course, *m'shu.* You will ride heem coach."

"They got orders not to take passengers between stations, ain't they?"

"Ha! I will tell them you are my frien' . . . one beeg, hones' man. Thees way I will keep my job, and you will ride to Diamond Gulch. All is good."

"All is good," repeated Comanche John, spitting at the ash hopper. He seated himself and spread jackboots expansively. "Glad you know an honest Christian pilgrim when you see one. Share and share alike . . . that's my motto."

There was a slight dawn grayness along the horizon when iron-banded coach tires rattled over the quartzite rocks of the road and the Concord rolled up from the spruce-shadowed darkness. None of your old side-trail mud wagons—this coach was shiny and new, her leather springs creaking with payload, and there were six horses in the trees. The driver, Long Lash Henry Travers, bellowed something to Frenchy and climbed down, tossing the ribbons to an Indian hostler who had been asleep in the horse shed. He strode to the shack with the shotgun guard following him. They found tea and poured some, cursing the Frenchman because he hadn't furnished coffee.

"Got heem passenger," said Frenchy. "My frien', John Jones from Soapstone Gulch."

"Your friend?" Long Lash Henry peered at John's whiskered face. "If he's your friend, all right." He said to John: "But you'll have to ride atop the hurricane, because we're loaded like an Irishman on Saint Patrick's Day."

"Gents," quoth John, "no seat would please me more."

He climbed to the luggage rack, his back resting on a drummer's sample chest, jackboots dangling between guard and driver as the coach careened swiftly away behind six fresh horses.

After suitably cursing the road, the horses, and the quality of tobacco that season, Long Lash began whiling away the last weary hours of his drive by singing in a corroded voice.

Comanche John rode to Beaverhead
In the fall of 'Sixty-Three,
To rob the coach at Bannack
And the sluices at Lone Teepee;
He shot up Eldorado
Chased the sheriff up a tree,
A faster man with six-guns
You seldom ever see.

The guard shifted his shotgun and grumbled: "I wish you'd quit singin' that damned doggerel. It makes me nervous."

"Didn't reckon a guard like Max Jobel would worry about old Comanche John."

"If he tries to rob this coach, I'll give you material for the last verse of that danged song. I'll let him have four ounces of number two buck right betwixt the eyes."

Max Jobel slapped his Eight-Gauge shotgun and squinted around at the passing shadows. He rolled with the motion of the coach for a while, his ribs jostling John's jackboot. He turned then, fixing John in a professionally suspicious gaze.

"What's your line, stranger?"

"Ever since the year o' 'Forty-Nine, I wandered along the wild frontier relievin' the weary pilgrim of his load. Share and share alike, that's my motto."

The guard mumbled something. He kept glancing from time to time at John's face. "I seen you some place before."

"Could be."

"You weren't down at Yaller Jacket last year?"

"Not me. Last year I was at Lewiston, helpin' conduct a mission."

Long Lash Henry looked startled. "A mission! You ain't a sky pilot?"

"You see in me," proclaimed John reverently, "practically a man o' the cloth, and I don't mean that green cloth they put atop cyard tables, neither."

Max Jobel said: "If you're a Bible-shouter, it seems damn' peculiar you'd be packin' two Navy sixes. And when you clumb up, I sort of imagined I saw notches in 'em."

"Reckon you never got far in Scriptures, brother, iffen you don't recollect how an old rangy-tang by the handle of Jeremiah hauled out his muzzle-loader and cut loose on a couple of robber's-roost gamblin' camps named Sody and Gomorrah. Well, sir, anything that's good enough for old Jeremiah is good enough for me."

"Hallelujah!" responded Long Lash Henry, pulling back on the brake handle to slow the coach's descent to a ford of the creek. It rolled through with cold mountain water making a hissing gurgle between the spokes, then he maneuvered the horses as they drew the coach one wheel at a time up the waist-high bank beyond.

John chewed and watched the portion of the guard's craggy face that was visible beneath the brim of his sheared-beaver sombrero. It was obvious that the guard knew his business. He leaned forward tensely at the crossing, the shotgun tilted forward, watching the close-growing rose brambles for sign of trouble.

The cañon narrowed. There was a sheer wall on one side and the creek on the other with barely room for the road between. It widened where a side cañon entered. There was a grove of trembly leafed aspen trees with the road winding in and out. Another steep ford, and another. The cañon was widening. Up ahead, John could see a pillar of rock and timber rising in a mass of solid shadow behind it. His pony waited in that timber.

"Gents," said John apologetically, "I'm afraid I'll have to ask you to halt this yere coach."

Long Lash spun around, and stared into the muzzles of two Navy Colts.

He froze to the ribbons, pulling back. He was bringing the leaders up fast with the wheelers and swing team overrunning them. It was a trifle downhill with no brake applied. The overloaded coach was rolling too fast.

"I wouldn't advise you to make that kind of mistake," said John.

If Long Lash had any idea of spilling the coach, he changed his mind at the steely sound of the words. Leather brake shoes ground on tires. The guard, Jobel, had not made a move, hadn't looked around, but just sat, hunched forward a trifle, the shotgun between his knees, barrel pointed straight up.

John spoke: "Drop the shotgun overboard. Keep your hand off the triggers."

"All right," Jobel answered through his teeth, still looking straight down the black roadway.

John's voice: "Take it slow."

Max Jobel lifted the gun with his right hand gripping the barrel. The barrel was still straight up. He slowly slid it down, turning it a trifle sidewise. Holding it that way, there was no possible way his fingers could get to the triggers.

There was a nail on the footrest of the high seat. He let it slide inside the trigger guard, twisted the barrel back, aiming behind his shoulder, directly at the spot from which Comanche John's voice had come. The shotgun leaped and roared, sending a blast of flame and buckshot from its Eight-Gauge barrel.

John had moved at the final instant. Jobel swung around, twisting the gun. Only one barrel had fired. He was trying to bring the nail to bear on the other trigger. John's right hand Navy traveled in a short, descending arc, the barrel struck, padded by Jobel's beaver hat. The guard let go the shotgun and pitched head foremost, striking the wheel and landing shoulder first on the ground.

Crash of the shotgun had started the horses forward, snorting, eyes rolling, pulling at cross-purposes. The coach rolled crazily through rock and scrub timber. Men were cursing inside—a woman screamed. John clung to the hurricane rail, Navies still in his hands.

The coach finally came to a stop, tilting steeply. There was a rattle from a door handle.

John's voice went over the side: "I got two Navies up hyar. One for each side. It mightn't be too healthy for the first two or three that comes out."

The handle did not rattle again.

"Thar's a strongbox in the boot," John said to Long Lash. "Just cinch your ribbons 'round the hand brake and toss it on the ground. I'll get down after it, turn around, and pick up your guard. He'll want somethin' for his headache when he gets to Diamond Gulch, and, if he's still worried about whar he seen me before, tell him I met him in a professional way three years ago near the town of Yuba City, Californy."

The strongbox was not heavy. John had no trouble carrying it uphill on his shoulder to the spot where Patches was tethered. He tied it behind the saddle with a strip of whang leather and rode uphill across rocks where trailing would be hard. Dawn was making streaks of pink and orange across the vast foothill country to the east when he dismounted, tossed the strongbox down, and smashed the twin locks with two expert shots from a Navy six.

He dumped out its contents. Papers in sealed packets from the express company—no value in those. He would leave them on the express platform. Some letters bearing registry seals. He'd leave those, also. The only other article was a packet addressed to John B. Enfield, Enfield & Mecklin, Diamond Gulch, M.T. It bore the seal of the Planters Bank, St. Louis.

He opened the package. It contained greenbacks in tightly bound mint packets. There was more than fifteen thousand. It totaled twenty-two thousand four hundred. That was fifteen thousand actual value, due to the depreciation of the greenback. He looked again at the name and address. John B. Enfield—that would be Field Macklin's partner in the coach line. It was beginning to make sense.

"Yep," he said, "it looks like John B. Enfield was gettin' himself a hand offen a cold deck."

He rode cross-country to Diamond Gulch with the banknotes stuffed in a buckskin saddlebag. It was shorter that way, and he arrived in town in time to see the stagecoach roll to a stop before the Enfield & Mecklin barns. A crowd instantly started to gather. Even at that dawn hour robbery news traveled fast. He rode downhill. The Mexican hostler wasn't around. He unsaddled the pony himself, and making no special effort at concealment he went downhill, carrying the saddlebag under his arm. He crossed a deep trench where Chinese were moving gravel in wheelbarrows and passed among a clutter of outhouses to the rear of the parson's mission.

It was cool and dim inside. He tossed the saddlebag in a corner, pulled off his jackboots. He was sound asleep on a wooden bench when the parson came.

"There was a coach robbed!" the parson announced in his parrot voice, glaring down on him.

John rolled to a sitting position, blinking his eyes. "Don't look at me. What coach was it?"

"You know what coach it was! The coach from Benton."

"*From* Benton? Hell, Parson, I'm better eddicated than that. Nobody but a Piegan squaw would rob an *incoming* coach. What would you think I was lookin' for . . . black-eyed beans and callyco?"

"You were lookin' for greenbacks."

"Them paper things the Union's been printin'? Parson, I can think of only one good use for greenbacks. Anyhow, what makes you so sure it was me? Why not Whisky Anderson? Or Muddy Jack Blue? Them highwaymen ain't been hung yet."

"The driver said it was you. Said he'd been robbed by Comanche John."

"Just wanted to play the hero, claimin' to be robbed by somebody famous. Thought maybe a poet would build his name inside another verse to my song. Why, I recollect one time they had me robbin' a coach at Virginny City and a sluice at Yellow Jacket two hundred mile away both on the same afternoon."

That was true, of course. A man gets a reputation like Comanche John's and every drunken prospector that loses his poke playing euchre with a Chinaman will come in claiming he's been robbed at the point of a gun by the most notorious man he can think of. The parson turned away. His eyes fell on the stuffed saddlebag.

"What's that?"

"Looks mighty like what us boys used to call a buckskin saddlebag." John yawned.

"Where'd it come from?"

"I tossed her thar when I came in last night."

The parson hefted it, untied the thongs. One of the packets of greenbacks came open, and the stiff new oblongs of paper spilled like cottonwood leaves in autumn. He sighed. This evidence of John's return to evil seemed to sadden more than anger him. Wearily he gathered them, put them back, and, with saddlebag under his arm, started for the door.

"Hold on. Whar ye goin'?"

"Out to give this money back."

"Like the devil ye are." John seized him by the front of his homespun jerkin and let him struggle a while. The parson had a wiry strength, and he was hard to hold. "Now listen. I didn't steal that money. Didn't I tell ye last night I was workin' for Field Mecklin? Well, that was the job. Stoppin' a Mecklin coach and liftin' the strongbox. *His* strongbox. I didn't tell you last night because it was the first honest job o' work I've had in fifteen year, and I didn't want you draggin' out your black Book and findin' out it was contrary to Levictus, chapter six, stanza fourteen, and six to one on the case cyards." The parson seemed curious to hear more, so John let him go. "Though I'll admit I had that shotgun guard fooled into thinkin' it was the real thing."

"You're lyin' to me!"

"No, I ain't, Parson," John said placidly. "However, I'll admit bein' party to somethin' that looks might-ee underhanded. You see . . . that package o' money was addressed to John Enfield."

"Ha!" cried the parson, eyes wide. He discarded his idea of going outside. Instead, he carried the saddlebag over and hid it beneath the pulpit. He came back saying—"Ha!"—all over again. "Well, can't you see?" he demanded.

"I'm beginning to see I had a mighty long horseback ride for nothin'," John grumbled.

"Can't you see why he wanted you to rob that coach? Old man Enfield died, and, since then, I hear tell Mecklin has been tryin' to buy out his end. Young Jack Enfield's been having a time for himself makin' this north leg of the route pay out. Losin' that money would like as not put him right up Skunk Crick without a paddle." He strode to the door. "I'm goin' out to find young Jack Enfield . . . and, by grab, you better keep your fingers offen that money."

"Glory be," breathed John. "Glory, glory be."

III

Jack Enfield was not in Diamond Gulch. The stage office reported him to be in Last Chance. John watched the parson ride down the gulch trail with the buckskin saddlebag. He cursed in selected words from the English, Spanish, Comanche tongues, then curled up and slept until late afternoon when he arose for a dinner of cold, boiled buffalo jerky. It was about dark then, so he tilted his slouch hat over his eyes and found himself a comfortable loafing spot against the back wall of the Confederate States Saloon.

He barely had his chew of blackstrap warmed up when Field Mecklin strode through the door. Mecklin seemed to be calm, but the rage that filled him was shown in his tense, bloodless lips—in the bleak shine of his eyes. He walked close and hissed through set teeth: "I thought I told you to leave the country when you got that money! Do you realize there were a half dozen on that coach who might recognize you? They'll have the vigilance committee. . . ."

"Might-ee nice o' you to worry about my health." John chewed.

"I don't give a good almighty damn about the state of your health. I'd gladly turn you over to that vigilance committee . . . provided they'd strangle you before you had a chance to talk."

John hee-hawed and beat dust from a leg of his homespun pants.

"Keep still, you fool." Mecklin in his anger had gone tense. He was not used to having people defy him. Veins stood out along his forehead. He kept nervously rubbing the palms of his hands just over the ivory butts of those two Smith & Wesson pistols.

John remained slouched, tilted on the hind legs of his chair. He chewed as before, but his eyes had become gray slits in his leather-brown face.

There was someone outside the door. Mecklin's face told him that, although he'd have known it anyway. The man wouldn't have come without his gun crew. John thumped forward in his chair and scraped it to one side to place Mecklin between himself and the door. The door opened almost immediately and Baldy—the Yellow Jacket gunman—sauntered in. He went over by the faro spread and stood, one shoulder resting on the wall, hands near guns, watching John with his long, predatory face. Blackie Andros came in a moment later. It must have been planned because he walked directly to a spot far enough toward the bar so John would have difficulty watching them both at the same time.

After observing this, John drawled: "You're likely to get caught right in the middle of this shoot-out, you know."

Mecklin said: "You saw who the money was addressed to, didn't you?"

"Now, my schoolin'. . . ."

"Jack Enfield knows you're in town. Suspicions that you are, anyway. His driver identified you. Enfield has a print-shop dodger with your picture."

"Tell Jackie boy to drop in and I'll buy him a drink."

"Get out. Get out of this town," Mecklin hissed.

"I'll get out when *I* want to." Comanche John spat a stream of tobacco juice accurately six inches short of Mecklin's polished boots. "When *I* want to. Without your advice."

Mecklin backed away, trembling with rage. After backing a third the distance across the room, he turned and strode outside, muttering something to Blackie Andros from the side of his mouth. Comanche John slouched forward toward the middle of the room. Andros watched him intently. He had one dirty thumb hooked in his belt. When John looked at Andros, the back of his head was turned toward Baldy.

It looked like the bald gunman's chance. He moved his hand toward his gun, forgetting the possibility of his movement being revealed in the back-bar mirror.

John did not turn. There was a sag in one shoulder, a twist of his arm, the heavy concussion of a gun. To an onlooker it would almost seem that the long Navy Colt had spun out on its own volition.

He had fired, aiming across his waist. The slug slammed Baldy back. His gun was unholstered, but he'd had no chance to aim. His eyes were off focus. He struck a card table and his knees gave out, spilling him face foremost across the rough floor.

John scarcely looked at him. His whiskered jaw still revolved around the chew of tobacco. Blackie Andros was bent in a gunfighter's crouch, hands hovering over the butts of his guns. He did not move. With extreme slowness he relaxed. His face, deeply cleft by its tomahawk scar, was at once frightened and cruel. He lifted his hands clear of his guns—kept them high.

The gunshot and sudden death had brought silence to the room. The silence hung for several seconds, broken only by the *scrape* of boots, the *creak* of chairs, as card players changed positions.

John said to Blackie Andros: "You ain't changed since the old days down in Californy, have ye, Blackie? Once a coward, always a coward, I say." He looked around at the others. "What do you think, boys? Did you see the bald varmint go for his gun?"

"Sho' he did," the faro dealer said in his Southern drawl. "He went for his gun, only the whiskered gent was too quick."

John slid the Navy back in its holster. He walked to the door, booted it open, and went outside.

The evening was cool with mountains silhouetted by a star-filled sky. He saw Field Mecklin, standing on the pole sidewalk before the Jones & Stuart freight lines office. He made a sudden start on seeing that it was Comanche John who came out. There was no doubt that he had heard the single gunshot and thought as a matter of course that John with his incriminating knowledge had been silenced.

John called in a voice just loud enough to reach across the narrow street: "Your man's inside! The bald one. Maybe you'd like he should have a fittin' Christian burial. If ye do, I'll arrange it. Sort of a sideline o' mine."

Mecklin's face wore its mask of suppressed rage. He moved as though to step from the walk—and checked himself. His hands hovered over the ivory revolver butts, but he didn't draw, not even when John turned his back and slouched down the succession of high and low platform sidewalks that fronted that side of the gulch street.

John knew that Mecklin was still watching him. He walked a hundred yards down the street, entered a hurdy-gurdy house where miners were raising dust from the floor, doing a California variety of polka with gaudily dressed girls at a dollar a dance.

He left by the back door, cut back along a hill trail among shanties and wickiups to the rear door of the mission.

There was no light inside. He felt his way through the bench-cluttered darkness, located flint and steel on the table, made sparks on tinder. The tinder flamed up, and he lit a candle.

He sensed rather than heard the movement behind him. He started around, and his muscles froze at the sound of a pistol hammer clicking back.

A voice he had never heard before said: "Put up your hands."

"Sure thing," drawled John. "Just take it calm." He lifted his hands, then turned slowly.

A young man with a pair of intent blue eyes was facing him

with a Navy six held steadily, aimed at his heart. The hammer was back, and the young man's finger rode the trigger.

"It don't take much to set one o' them things off, you know."

His finger remained where it was. "Yes, I know."

"Playing a little seven-up. Jerky and dumplings in the pot."

"I'm looking for my money."

"You must be Jack Enfield."

"I am." He jiggled the muzzle of the Navy. "Where is it?"

"It's hid, and, if you set off that powder keg by accident, I doubt you'll ever find it."

Enfield seemed to be thinking this over. He was a good-looking lad, about twenty-two, six feet or a trifle more with a clean grace about him. His skin was deeply tanned, but it lacked the leathery cast of John's who was fifteen or twenty years older. A lock of straw-colored hair hung on his forehead from beneath the brim of his cavalry hat.

"Unfasten your gun belts," he said. Then, when John started to lower both hands: "One hand's enough."

John's black whiskers parted in a smile. He kept one hand high, while the other unfastened the belts. The heavy, holstered Navies would have carried them to the floor, only he caught them between his knees. He picked up belts, holsters, guns in one big handful and thrust them forward.

They were momentarily in front of Enfield's gun. He shifted a trifle. For a fraction of time his aim was off. John swung a looped belt with a slight twist of the hand and caught the gun barrel, jerking it aside. With an accompanying movement John booted one of the heavy log benches against Enfield's knees.

The young man was twisting to one side when the bench struck him. He was driven backward. There were spurs on his boots, and one of the big Spanish rowels caught in the split-pole floor. He went down on his side, catching himself with an outflung left arm.

The pistol was still in his hand. He twisted it over, trying to aim over his thigh, but John had leaped the bench. His foot swung, connecting with Enfield's wrist, sending the gun bounding across the floor. John jerked one of his own Navies from its holster. He didn't bother to point it. Just stood, watching Enfield good-humoredly, making sure he didn't make a dive to retrieve his gun.

"Why don't you shoot?" Enfield cried. "You have me where you want me!"

"Why don't I? Maybe because I got me a hunk o' religion. Maybe because I like you a heap better'n your partner."

Enfield got up. The bench had bruised his knee, and he hobbled on it. John took time to buckle his Navies around his waist. When he was through, he picked up Enfield's pistol, released the hammer, and tossed it to him.

"Put this away, son."

The young man caught the gun and stood staring at it a few seconds before holstering it. John freshened his chew of tobacco and said: "You'll get your money back, only my partner rode off with it thinkin' he'd find you in Last Chance."

"I don't understand. Why did you rob . . . ?"

"*Rob?* I'm as innocent of robbery as a babe unborn. I was framed into liftin' that money box. Framed by Field Mecklin. Your partner."

Enfield shook his head. The hardness in his eyes showed that John's words had only confirmed some suspicions he'd had all along. He said: "Field Mecklin isn't my partner. The firm of Enfield and Mecklin never was a partnership. My father owned a stage line between Salt Lake and Soda Wells.

When he sold it to Ben Holladay, he made an agreement with Mecklin to put in a line between Bannack and Last Chance, connecting with Mecklin's line that was already operating between Bannack and Salt Lake. Later my dad decided to connect with Diamond Gulch and Fort Benton. He had trouble with Mecklin over that. He wanted to give Dad the line from Last Chance to here, and take over the leg to Fort Benton himself. That would give him a stranglehold on both ends, so Dad refused. So he started running coaches despite Mecklin's objections. Six weeks ago Dad got killed in a runaway . . . I suppose you heard. I came up from Bannack to take over. That's when I found out how far we were in debt."

"To Mecklin?"

"To Gerstenhover of the Last Chance Bank chiefly. He'd lent forty-eight thousand. There's a payment due. I need this money to cover it. It was some I had coming from my mother's estate. Mecklin has been trying to buy this north end of the line, so I suppose he thought losing this fifteen thousand would force my hand."

"You told Mecklin you were expecting the money?"

"No."

"Gerstenhover told him."

"Gerstenhover's not that kind of a man."

"He's a banker, ain't he? Listen to me, son . . . you'll never find such varmints in the road agent business as you will inside of banks."

Enfield fingered the butt of his Navy, his face craggy, eyes narrowed.

"You're aimin' to hunt out Mecklin, I suppose," John said.

"What if I am?"

"Take it calm, son. Tangle with him tonight and he'll likely make wolf bait of ye."

★★★★★

They were to wait for the parson to return. John leaned back on a stool, feet on the table, intending to sleep. Jack Enfield stood up and quietly went outside.

John watched with one eye open. When the door closed, he took down his boots and followed. The young man went across the street and inside the stage company office. When five minutes passed with no more sign of him, John decided he had gone to bed. He went back to the mission and lay down.

He was awakened by three pistol shots, one close on the other. There was nothing unusual about a little shooting in Diamond Gulch, but he got up, loosened his Navies in their holsters, and went outside.

A knot of spectators was gathered near the lighted entrance to the two-story Territorial Hotel. Two men came down the steps supporting a third man between them. Light fell on them from a saloon window. The wounded man was Jack Enfield. John knew one of the others—Long Lash Henry Travers.

Enfield was scarcely recognizable. His face looked pulpy as though someone had struck him repeatedly with a club so that blood oozed from his pores. His eyes were bruised and swelling shut. His left leg was wounded and the trouser leg stiffening from blood.

"You," muttered Long Lash Henry, stopping abruptly when he recognized Comanche John.

"Don't get hostile. Your boss is a friend o' mine."

Sound of John's voice penetrated to Enfield's slugged brain. His eyes came to focus through puffed lids. "Maybe I should have taken your advice," he said with an attempt at smiling.

"I take it you found Mecklin."

"At the Territorial Hotel. His men tried to get me in the back. Guess I was lucky. Just a leg wound. I couldn't fight three of 'em." He went into his slugged stupor again.

Long Lash said: "It was Mecklin. Got him down and booted him in the face. Every time his boot struck, the blood flew." He called Mecklin a string of vile words, then said defensively: "I couldn't do nothin'. One man can't fight a dozen gunmen and that's how many Mecklin has around if you counted 'em all."

"Better get the lad to the barn," John said, tilting his head toward the stage office.

Young Jack Enfield's injuries didn't seem so bad once the blood was washed away. The bullet wound had cut deeply through the flesh of his thigh, but it had not touched bone or large artery. John got the caked blood washed away and bound it with a poultice of hot sage leaves.

"Best thing that ever happened to him," John said, thumbing at the wound. "It'll keep him down till he has a chance to think things over. He's no artist with a gun. I found that out tonight."

IV

The parson returned next afternoon with the saddlebag of greenbacks, and the day following Jack Enfield felt good enough to limp to Gerstenhover's office and make a twelve thousand dollar payment on his loan—or eighteen thousand in greenbacks, for the loan, like all along the gold frontier, had been made in gold equivalent.

Gerstenhover was a medium tall, heavy German from St. Louis with intensely blue eyes and a good-natured face. He was no doubt shrewder than he gave the appearance of being.

"I vas so afraid for you, Jackie," he said, counting the greenbacks. "Yah. After I hear of stagecoach robbery, I am really poor man, you understand." He dipped a quill pen and wrote a receipt, signing his name with an intricate assortment of broad strokes and flourishes. Afterward, he put the money inside a tin box that he locked, and in turn placed in a drawer of his ornate walnut desk that he also locked. "*Ach!* . . . me and my shoestring business! Never should I lend to my friends. With enemies . . . those if they do not pay it is good to foreclose, yah. But mine friends! If you do not pay, what is there left for me to do. I have mine indebtedness, too."

John had been standing in the door. He slouched over and sat on the edge of the ornate desk. "If you get too hard up, you could always buy a year's grubstake by cashing in that rock in your necktie."

"Ho! You just joke." Gerstenhover touched the big diamond in his tie. "You make joke. This is just cheap bauble. I am poor man." Gerstenhover leaned back, drumming the desk with stubby pink fingers. He looked at John's whiskered face. "I haff seen you some place before?"

"Not 'less you've been to church lately."

Gerstenhover chuckled deep in his thick throat. "I haff heard that black-whiskered man robbed Fort Benton coach. Maybe Comanche John. Yah, that was name . . . Comanche John? I have also heard this Comanche John was wanted by Bannack vigilantes."

"You ain't accusin' me o' bein' a varmint like that!"

"Ho! . . . like you I only make joke. Any friend of Jackie is a friend of mine."

They went outside, Enfield folding his receipt, putting it in a Spanish leather wallet.

"Bank-keepin' high-grader!" growled John.

"He was my father's best friend," Enfield said in mild

reproach. "You're just suspicious of bankers in general. Gerstenhover's a good Dutchman."

"How do ye aim to get the next twelve thousand?"

"Out of the company profits."

"Is the coach business *that* good?" John asked incredulously.

"It's that good . . . if everything goes right."

Everything did not go right. Next night the coach from Last Chance rolled in riddled with bullets, the shotgun guard lying dead on the floor inside, and the money gone. Two days later the outbound coach for Benton was robbed of a thousand-ounce gold shipment. Then, at the end of the week, Field Mecklin announced inauguration of an extension to his line so it would reach both Last Chance and Diamond Gulch.

Mecklin next journeyed to Fort Benton where he was reported making an agreement with Craft Burroughs, a big-time Missouri River fur trader and steamboat owner. He returned, and the following week the *Territorial News* from Last Chance published a story predicting a "new, fast, one-company service under the Mecklin banner joining the steamboats of the Missouri with the Ben Holladay coach line to California."

In the meantime, trouble for Enfield coaches continued. It became difficult to hire men, even at double wages, so Comanche John hired out, riding shotgun with Long Lash Henry Travers. He returned, tired and dusty after his third trip, and paused for a bottle of beer at the Confederate States saloon. A skinny, red-whiskered man grinned and sidled up to him.

"Well, John!"

The familiar voice made him spin around with a bellow of delight. "You old he-wolf!" John roared, stamping his bootheels. "Ye mangy old he-wolf. I heered them stranglin' vigilantes got ye over at Hellgate a month ago."

"Why, they had some idees, but they didn't have fast enough hosses to go with 'em, so here I be."

They pumped each other's hands—Comanche John and Whisky Anderson.

"You hear that song they writ about us?" John asked, and sang.

Comanche John rode to I-dee-ho
In the year of 'Sixty-Two
With a pal named Whisky Anderson
And one named Henry Drew. . . .

"I heard her."

"What ye doin' here?" John's eyes narrowed down. "We been havin' a considerable of coach robbery lately. Enfield coaches, that is. Mecklin's outfits seem to be makin' her all right."

"You know my business, John. Gold is whar you find it, and, if I happen to find it on an Enfield coach. . . ."

"I been ridin' shotgun on that Benton run now and again," John said significantly.

"So I heered." Whisky Anderson peered intently into John's eyes. "You must have a mighty good idee what coaches it would pay to rob."

"Mebby, but that's not why I'm ridin' her."

Whisky Anderson chuckled, peering with squinty gray-green eyes as though there was always more on his mind than ever reached his lips. "John, you was born a ring-tailed roarer, and it's hard to learn an old wolf to tend sheep, as the sayin' goes. I know how you stand here in Diamond Gulch, how you been goin' to church and hobnobbin' with stage-coach owners, but I knowed ye in I-dee-ho, and before that in

Californy. Hell, man, your reputation wouldn't let you be a Sunday-goin' Samaritan even if you et one o' them Bibles, paper, horsehide cover, and all."

"Just what have you got on your mind, Whisky?"

"Gold."

"Whar?"

"On a stagecoach. One o' them Enfield Concords. The one headed for Benton tomorrow morning."

John had heard of no gold shipment going out, but, of course, he'd only that hour returned after a three-day absence from camp. "Could be. But it ain't good sense, comin' to me. Likely I'll be ridin' guard on that coach." John nudged him and chuckled. "I'm a mighty potent shotgun guard. Man that's been on the wrong side of the road as often as I have sort of gets so he senses whar the danger is, and which o' the road agents he ought to shoot first, which one second, and so on. The delicate touch, you understand."

"You wouldn't shoot *me!*"

John scratched his whiskers. "Well, I dunno. You see, I've reformed. Used to be I just took gold wherever I found her. But I quit that. True, I still lift a poke here or thar, but generally from varmints. Not from good lads like Jack Enfield." Then he asked: "Who sent you around for me?"

"Nobody. Blackie Andros said he needed a couple more men, and, when I heered you was in the country. . . ."

"Blackie Andros!" John spat to get the taste of the name out of his mouth. "That polecat! You look out for him or he'll make vigilante bait out of you for the ree-ward like he did that Ho Parker gang down in the Sierras."

After a couple of drinks, John clomped up the sidewalk through the fresh coolness of the mountain evening, finding Jack Enfield in his invoice-cluttered office at the stage station.

"Hello," Enfield said.

"Gold shipment going out tomorrow, I hear."

The question apparently startled the young man. He nodded: "Why, yes. But I'd like to know how in the devil you found out."

"Road agent told me."

"Who was he?"

"Oh, one o' Blackie Andros's men. Came around to hire me."

Jack Enfield thought it over, leaning back, eyes on the rough-board wall. His mind was running through the various men in his employ, wondering which had furnished the information. He said: "It's a thousand-ounce shipment we have to get to Benton before the *Cree Chief* sails for Saint Louis. Skip Fraser's gold. The clean-up from his Royal Crown placer over at Last Chance. On its way here now. We were going to store it overnight and toss it on the coach tomorrow morning. Long Lash Henry's coach with you riding shotgun. Did this, ah, road agent friend of yours know you'd come and tell me?"

"He has a fair idee."

"Then we'll put the gold through on schedule. They'll expect us to delay it now that we've been warned."

John wasn't exactly sure that this thinking was as tricky as Enfield considered it to be. He climbed the rocky path to the mission with face unusually troubled. The parson was lighting up the grease dips, getting ready for his nightly meeting. Things weren't going well for the parson, either. He'd been getting no more than two dozen of Diamond Gulch's rough citizens to attend, and half of those were generally drunks, attracted by the singing, who immediately started bellowing for likker and the girls.

"How's business with the sinners?" John asked, getting the jack and pulling his boots off.

"Doin' a good funeral business," moaned the parson, "but a funeral's a mighty tardy place for the savin' of souls from the fires of eternal damnation."

"Amen and hallelujah!" intoned Comanche John. "And the way this stagecoach business is headed, you'll have plenty funerals more."

The meeting was over before midnight, and John had been snoring for two hours when Whisky Anderson prowled inside, calling his name. John lighted a candle.

"What d'ye want!" he asked. "Go ahead. You can talk in front o' the parson."

"I just wanted to let you know that I didn't tell Blackie or anybody else about the talk we had. And as for me, I said he could go to hell with his stick-up!"

"Amen!" quoth the parson, standing like a plucked buzzard with bare legs sticking from his nightshirt. "Another convert from the paths of wretchedness. Another gun-packin' pilgrim for the army o' the Lord."

"I ain't gone that far," said Whisky uncharitably. "I just couldn't see me linin' myself up with Blackie Andros on one side o' me and Comanche John on the other. That was too much like ridin' a powder wagon with a bob-tailed fuse."

When he was gone, John dressed and crossed to the stage station. There was a candle burning inside but no one in sight. He tried the door. It was barred. He rapped. Max Jobel was sitting guard in the darkened room next to the office. He saw who it was and walked over with a surly attitude to lift the bar. Jobel had never forgiven Comanche John for bashing him that night in Longknife Cañon, and he'd have gone to Buffalo Browers, head of the vigilantes, the first day if it hadn't been for Enfield's order not to.

"Enfield around?" John asked.

"In his room," Jobel grunted. He backed up in a way that blocked the stairs, sawed-off shotgun across his arm. "What do you want of him?"

"That," said John, "happens to be none of your damned business." When Jobel still blocked the way, John roared: "Git out o' my way!"

Jobel edged over enough to let him pass. John stood where he was. He had survived well along this wild gunman's country, and his survival was partly due to an instinct for danger. That instinct led him to suspect a charge of buckshot from Jobel's gun when his back was turned.

Jack Enfield had awakened at the commotion and walked barefoot to the head of the stairs. "What's going on?"

Jobel put down the shotgun and answered in a surly, defensive voice: "You told me not to let anybody in."

"That's all right." Then to John: "Come on up."

John went inside the dinky room, closing its plank door before telling Enfield of Whisky Anderson's visit.

"You believe him?" Enfield asked. "They could have sent him back to tell you that just so we'd think we were safe and send the gold through tomorrow."

"Could be. Only Whisky's always been honest with me."

Enfield thought it over.

"Are you sending her through?"

"No. Chances are he's telling the truth. I think they'll make a try for it. I'll send the gold through later in the week." He chuckled grimly. "Tomorrow, instead of gold, we'll give that gang the biggest damned surprise of their lives."

V

The Benton coach left at dawn with Long Lash and Comanche John on the high seat, but inside, instead of the usual payload, was Jack Enfield, Max Jobel, and the shotgun guard from the Virginia City end, a quiet man of middle age by the name of Quinlan.

They expected trouble in the timber of Diamond Gulch, or in Longknife Cañon, but the swing station at Frenchy's was reached without incident. Round-topped mountains with spotty timber lay beyond, then grassy hills, and, after that, prairie that stretched to a limitless, purple horizon. At intervals the coach would draw up to a dinky shanty and corrals for a change of horses, then it would roll on, keeping to schedule.

The home station at Sage Coulée was reached at late afternoon. At Sage there was a long log cabin with a dirt and pole roof, an extensive assortment of sheds and corrals, and a reservoir with its little lake and circling efflorescence of alkali that looked like spilled baking soda. Ordinarily Long Lash spent the night at Sage Station, but this time he merely ate the meal of beans and fried antelope that the stationkeeper's Blackfoot squaw placed on the table, and climbed inside with Enfield, Jobel, and Quinlan. The coach rolled on with the new driver, Dandy Dave Tilford, in the seat.

Darkness settled with thunder and black clouds rolling up from the prairie. Midnight found them on Shonkin Creek with the trail winding through cottonwoods, past a corral and half-completed log station being put up by Field Mecklin, then on to Rosard's trading post where a hundred-teepee encampment of Assiniboines could be seen by repeated lightning flashes. Scattering drops of rain fell, making an odor of wet dust. Dawn was breaking when they headed down the miles of bluff road to Fort Benton.

"Skunked!" growled Max Jobel in ill temper, dragging himself outside as the coach was hauled across the Missouri on a current-operated ferry. He said to Enfield: "Probably raided the station and took that gold as soon as we were out of the way."

Benton lay on the flats, uphill from warehouses and log docks where sternwheel riverboats were moored. There was little rest. Fresh horses were hitched, a new driver took over, express was piled in the rear boot and lashed to the top.

A young woman was waiting in the stage office when Jack Enfield went in. There was a trunk and several carpetbags on the floor at her feet. For a moment his eyes were blinded by the bright, dawn sunshine, then he saw that she was young, about average height, slim. What he saw over and above that was her fresh appearance, her unpainted beauty which a man gets to hungering for after spending a couple of years in the brawling boom camps of the gold frontier.

"You're with the coach company?" she asked in a voice pitched lower than most women.

"Yes, miss."

"I wanted passage on the Diamond Gulch coach. The agent said I'd have to wait and see. Something about a company load he hadn't expected. I was left behind yesterday because there wasn't room."

Enfield said mildly: "The down-going coaches are always crowded. Sometimes the space is spoken for a week in advance."

"But he told me I could get passage today."

"I'm not the agent. It's up to the agent to distribute space."

She was becoming angry—he could tell that by the way her slim hands gripped the handle of her parasol, by the tight line of her lips. "Sir! I'm not willing to spend a second night in this . . . this. . . ."—she gestured around her at the frontier town.—"I'm not going to be left here another day waiting for passage. If I'm not given a seat on this coach, I'll take it up personally with Mister Field Mecklin."

He said gently: "Mister Mecklin is no longer associated with this stage line."

"Your sign says. . . ."

"It says Enfield and Mecklin. We'll have to paint a new one. It is now the Enfield stage line. I should have told you . . . I'm Jack Enfield."

"Oh! Well, I'll not beg for a seat on your coach."

He decided to smile. It was a good smile, and it quieted her anger. "I wouldn't want you to beg. There's no reason why you should. I run a business, and you're a customer. I guess, if you want passage to Diamond Gulch, you can have it. In fact, if you wanted passage yesterday, it should have been given to you. It's always been our policy to favor women . . . your kind of women. We don't often get a chance to haul 'em."

She colored a trifle at reference to her "kind of women". She said: "Isn't Mister Mecklin in Diamond Gulch now?"

"I haven't seen him for a week, miss."

Her brows drew together over her nose. It was a small nose, perfectly formed, with just a few freckles across its bridge.

He said: "The coach goes on to Last Chance. We don't have a decent hotel in Diamond Gulch, but there's an extra fine place they just finished building in Last Chance. If you're afraid somebody won't be waiting for you. . . ."

"My stepfather and mother will be in Diamond Gulch.

Mister and Missus Gerstenhover."

He nodded. "I saw Mister Gerstenhover only yesterday." He added: "Mister Gerstenhover was one of my father's best friends."

The information seemed to place them on a different plane. "I'm sorry," she said. "Not about . . . I'm sorry I was so unpleasant."

"It's not easy for a girl to travel in this country. Not when she's alone."

She introduced herself then. She was Bess McGrail. Her widowed mother had married Gerstenhover in St. Louis and left with him on a journey whose original destination was Sacramento, but had finally ended in Diamond Gulch. For the past two years Bess McGrail had lived with her uncle, Colonel Stephen McGrail of the Union Army, stationed at St. Joseph, Missouri, but he had insisted on her departure because of the unsettled conditions caused by the invasion of Confederate General Sterling Price from Arkansas.

It seemed strange—this girl seeking safety in a wild frontier, terrorized on one side by Blackfeet, and on the other by organized gangs of bandits. She did not mention Field Mecklin again.

The coach set out in half an hour. It was one of the big, new Concords made to squeeze in as many as ten or eleven passengers, but one of the cross-seats had been removed to make room for rush mail and express, so it carried nine with Long Lash clinging to the hurricane.

They passed the upcoming coach at Sage Station and paused at that place about dark where Long Lash took over, piloting the coach through moonlit night.

Hours passed, and Comanche John dozed. He jerked awake with the sudden movement of Long Lash as he swung the lead team from the road.

"What the devil?" The words were bumped out of John as he clutched with one hand, barely keeping his seat as the coach started a wild, rolling ride across the hummocky prairie.

"Gun shine yonder," Long Lash answered. "Beyond that sand rock."

The sand rock was a projecting strata with the road winding closely around it. At the right was a little swale covered spottily with sage funneling into the upper end of a dry wash. It was the protection of the dry wash that Long Lash was trying to reach.

Men were shouting from outside. Questions no one bothered to answer.

Comanche John had the shotgun between his knees. He thrust it muzzle down in its wagon scabbard, taking instead one of those new breech-loading German rifles that used .34 caliber metallic ammunition. He rolled belly down on the top of the coach, finding a spot between a box of Baker Company time freight and the girl's lashed-down trunk.

Men were on the move back of the sand rock. It was less than a hundred yards away. He could see shadow, the gleam of gunmetal in moonlight. Men were on horseback, galloping across the swale, disappearing over the edge of the dry wash.

Long Lash saw they were cut off from the wash as he swung his team to the right. He was going to make a try for it with the sand rock on one side and the dry wash on the other.

A gun's high, angry crack asserted itself over the thunder of hoofs and coach wheels. John fired at its powder flash from atop the pitching coach. Other rifles cut loose from the sand rock—from the edge of the wash. Bullets tore splinters, thudded into the coach. John kept stuffing cartridges in the breech of the rifle, firing.

The horses were on a dead run. One of the swing team was

hit. The poor animal stumbled and went down, the wheel team piling over him.

The coach skidded halfway around, balanced for a moment on two wheels. Then, with a movement that seemed leisurely after the wild, pitching ride, it fell to its side.

Comanche John was flung face down in bunchgrass and sage. The rifle was gone—batted from his hands, but the Navies were safe. He drew, crouching on one knee.

Blackie Andros's voice came across the night, shouting orders. A horse and rider were in view at one end of the sand rock. Three more a second later. Then another group from the upper end of the natural fort.

John racked back the hammers. "Come on, ye yaller-gutted polecats!" he whooped. "It's Christmas time and we're servin' lead cranberries!"

The first four riders had fanned out, coming on the run. John held his fire as distance diminished. Then the Navies roared, rocking his hands. He fired twice more—once with each pistol.

One man was batted backward. He fell and was dragged by his foot, shoulders and arms flopping as they bounded along the ground. The man beside him spilled head foremost. Another rider drew his horse to a sliding stop and went galloping in flight. The other man was still coming on. He was clinging flat against the horse, using the animal's neck and head for protection. Moonlight shone on the short barrel of the shotgun he carried in one hand.

The horse veered, bringing the man to view. He turned, aiming the sawed-off. John's Navies roared, driving the man back so the sawed-off sent its shot roaring overhead. The fellow hit the ground and rolled almost to John's feet.

The other group of riders had swung away at the unexpected fury of the gunfire that was now coming from behind the coach. John backed to the coach, finding the shotgun. Only a couple of loads were left in his Navies. No use wasting them, shooting at gun flashes. A shotgun loaded with buck was another matter—a squaw gun like that did her own aiming.

One of the men in the dry wash had bellied up until he was only forty or fifty yards off. John waited for the flash of his gun. He caught the light of it against the front bead of the Eight-Gauge. The shotgun boomed, its recoil spinning John halfway around. He could hear the man's scream and sucking cry—could see him stumble into sight, torn by a half-dozen buckshot, and go face first to the prairie sod.

"Come on, ye back-shootin' bushwhackers!" John bellowed. "Come on a dozen more o' ye while I play a tune on this Californy calliope."

He sighted another flash and sent another charge that tore dust and sod from the edge of the wash without known result. "I wish the parson was hyar. Thar's nothin' like a splatter-gun with buck in her to catch up with a sinner and teach him the ways o' rightcousness."

It settled down to steady shooting, the coach pinned by crossfire. Long Lash Henry crouched by one of the dying horses, cursing the attackers. "I can abide killin' a man, but any man that assassinates a hoss is next kin to a blow snake."

John didn't answer. He was bellying across the ground, keeping the fallen coach between himself and the sand rock, finding concealment in sage clumps from the men in the dry wash. A little rise of earth hid him, then it was open ground for a dozen yards. Beneath him he could see the abrupt, six-foot descent to the wash, its bottom a tangle of sage and dry-pooled snakeweed. He slid down, digging heels in dry dirt.

"John?" said a voice close by in shadow.

"Yes," he grunted.

Evidently there was one of the bushwhackers named John. He could see no one. The man was beyond a bend in the steep bank. An instant later his shadow became visible. John waited, Navy ready. At the last instant the man seemed to realize this was not the "John" he expected. His gun shattered the air so close that bits of powder burned John's cheeks, but the man was flinging himself back at the same moment, and the bullet thudded in the dirt up the bank.

John stood with shoulders flattened, aiming a Navy at arm's length, ready for the next movement. He spoke. "I'm John, all right. I'm Comanche John, and I'm quite a hand at killin' dry-gulchers. Now listen careful, and I'll tell ye just what to do so you'll be around for flapjacks tomorrow mornin'. You toss your gun down, stick both hands out straight from that bank so I can see they're empty. Then come along so I can squint at your face."

Mention of that name, Comanche John, brought a singularly rapid response. The gun dropped. John picked it up, grunted with satisfaction to see there were four loads in it, and thrust it in the band of his homespuns. The man's hands were in sight, thrust horizontally.

"All right, Lazarus," quoth John, "ye can come forth now."

He looked at the man's long, loose-mouthed face. A saloon loafer from Diamond Gulch. "Don't shoot," he whined. "You promised."

"Whar's your boys?"

"Fisher and Alrod's up the gulch, Mex is dead."

"Good for him. You lead the way, and we'll see what we can do about Fisher and Alrod."

The loose-mouthed man led him through rattling snakeweed. He covered thirty or forty yards. A man spoke his name.

"Beggs?"

"Yeah." He walked on, prodded by John's Navies.

"Who were you talkin' to?"

John said: "Me, Comanche John. Just drop your implements o' destruction, gents, and put your continued existence down to the fact that this 'n' is one o' my charitable moods."

Shooting was intermittent from stagecoach and sand rock. Dawn was commencing to gray the stars.

"Enfield!" John called.

Enfield's voice: "Yes. Where are you?"

"Out hyar in the wash, trappin' skunks. Got three . . . t'other's a customer for the parson. You leave the gal and crawl over. Keep her behind the coach and she'll be safe enough."

"I can't leave. . . ."

"Bring her over. Then go back and do what ye damned please. They'll make wolf bait of you for sure if you stay there."

VI

Jack Enfield had awakened a moment before the coach commenced its wild ride, and he sensed instantly what was the matter. His first thought was of Bess McGrail, and he cursed himself for giving her passage. He expected her to scream, faint, weep, and do the other things expected of women in distress. But she did none of them.

Bullets ripped through the coach, three or four of them, and it was almost a relief when the vehicle rammed to a stop and crashed over. People were a tangled mass, trying to clamber from door and windows, but there was temporary safety in the thick, oak bottom.

Once outside she did not scrabble for cover as a couple of the male passengers did. She sat quite straight, her shoulder pressing his arm, watching him methodically aim and fire his pistol.

In response to John's suggestion, he took her across the open ground. There was no particular danger, coach and fallen horses obscuring them from the sand rock. It was only in the safety of the wash that she showed a sign of weakening. There she clutched tightly to Enfield's arm while repeated shudders ran through her body.

"These lads have been good enough to leave some hosses down the coulée," John drawled. "Get her down to Frenchy's. We'll put the run on the rest o' those boys, come daylight."

They were half-tamed Indian ponies. It was impossible for the girl to ride side-saddle, and she was not wearing a riding skirt.

"Go ahead," Enfield said. "This is no time for modesty."

He could sense the flush of her cheeks as he held the horse on short halter, looking the other way. After a couple of false movements, she mounted. He could tell that she'd ridden before.

"All right?"

"Yes," she whispered.

They rode together along the deepening bottom of the dry wash, then over its rim to the prairie.

Sounds of shooting had stopped. Dawn was casting a gray light over the bench land. They could make out the overturned coach with men standing near. The attackers were evidently gone.

"Should we go back?" Enfield asked.

"No." She laid her hand on his arm. "Please, I'd rather not."

He understood. She didn't want them to see her riding man-fashion.

They rode side-by-side as the prairie pinched out between foothills. The sun came up with warm, slanting rays. Frenchy's came in sight through scattered spruce timber.

Enfield dismounted, lifting Bess McGrail from her horse. She pushed herself away when he seemed to hold her a second, and spent some time smoothing her long, brown traveling skirt.

"What you must think of me!" she said.

"I think you are the prettiest girl I ever saw."

His words made her flush.

"You mustn't think anything of riding that way, miss. Out in this country girls ride just about the same as men." He pointed to the shack. "That's our swing station, yonder. Frenchy'll make tea and a bite o' breakfast. Rest of the boys should be along pretty soon. I'll ride to town and come back with a coach."

The relief coach arrived about noon with Enfield himself driving and heavy-set Gerstenhover in the high seat beside him. Gerstenhover lumbered down, opening his arms for the girl.

"*Ach,* mine Bess! Mine pretty Bess! If I was young man again would I marry your mama? I ask it . . . *nein.*"

She seemed pleased to see him. Enfield went to the door of the shack. He stopped abruptly, seeing a dead man on the floor. "Any more?" he asked John grimly.

"That long-eared drummer was nicked, but he ain't hurt like he pretends. If he is, let him gulp some o' that hoss medicine he's sellin'."

"Where are those men you caught in the dry wash?"

"Turned 'em loose." Then defensively: "I don't reckon I got the reputation to do much testifyin' before a vigilante committee."

★ ★ ★ ★ ★

The citizens of Diamond Gulch turned out three hundred strong to greet the coach. "Hear it was Comanche John's gang," somebody kept saying, over and over.

"Ought to hang the killin' pup," a prospector growled. "What's wrong with the vigilantes that they let a man like that operate?"

They forgot about Comanche John when the coach door opened and the girl stepped out, hand on Gerstenhover's arm. A lane opened through the crowd. Someone was pushing that way, tall, heavy-shouldered Field Mecklin.

"My dear!" he said, beaming. "Bess! If I'd only known. . . ."

"It's all right," she said, letting go her stepfather's arm and hurrying to meet him. She let him take both her hands.

He said: "But you said you'd take the Holladay coach to Fort Hall."

"Uncle Stephen thought the steamboat would be safer."

Enfield watched them. His face was tense, muscles knotted at the sides of his jaw. She had mentioned Mecklin at Fort Benton, but he thought him only a casual acquaintance. Obviously he was much more. Enfield turned away.

"You ain't going to let him have her?" John growled.

"She means nothing to me. I got her here safely."

"Mister Enfield!" He hesitated a moment before turning when she spoke. She was coming toward him. "I didn't thank you."

"It's all right. I should be apologizing for not giving better protection." He smiled through the thin line of his lips. "Competition is a little tough in the stagecoach business, you know."

Mecklin was following. He chose to ignore the remark. He spoke: "Old man! I'll never be able to thank you enough.

Miss McGrail is my future wife, you know." He spoke the words with booming sincerity. Mecklin was a good actor; even his eyes seemed grateful.

Gerstenhover said: "*Ach,* yes. Be friends, boys. Shake hands, yah? What is a little misunderstanding between gentlemen?"

"I'm not so sure," said Enfield, "that I'm a gentleman."

The gold went out on next morning's stage, reaching Benton without incident.

"They'll lie low for a while," Long Lash predicted, but he was wrong. Next morning the southbound coach to Last Chance was robbed of a four thousand dollar shipment.

"It's peculiar," Enfield said to the glum group in the stage office. "It's *damned* peculiar how they always know which stage to stop."

Comanche John felt several pairs of eyes, and he said: "I was in town yestiddy at the hour that coach was robbed, and I got the parson as witness."

"Nobody was accusing you," Enfield said sharply. "But somewhere there's a leak."

Next night, John was in the group of five that Enfield informed of the big shipment from Skip Fraser's mine that was slated for the Benton coach next day. The others were Buchanan, a driver, a shotgun guard named Munn, Max Jobel, and Long Lash Henry Travers.

"I've insured the shipment," Enfield said. "People are losing confidence in my coaches. After I've built a fair record, the regular insurance companies will take the risk, but as things stand now, the profit, or loss, will be mine. Losing this ten thousand dollar shipment would ruin me. That's why it has to get through. People are used to seeing the big ones go out with Jobel or John riding shotgun. For that reason I'm sending Munn, and Buchanan will drive. I think you others have earned a day off." Enfield turned and left the office.

After leaving the stage office, Comanche John stopped for one drink at the Confederate States, then he clomped down the sidewalk to the parson's. It was after midnight, and the old man was asleep. John simply walked through and out the rear door. Thus, reasonably sure that no one was following, he climbed along the mountainside, coming to Jobel's cabin from the rear. It was a dinky place of log, as much dugout as house. The reddish glow of a grease dip showed through an oiled-paper window. John hunkered in a clump of juniper, chewing tobacco, waiting. He had a hunch that Jobel was informing Mecklin, and, if so, Mecklin was liable to send a man up here.

After an hour the grease dip blinked out. John thought Jobel had gone to bed. He cursed a little and got up, shaking hitches from his knees. He crouched down quickly. The door had squeaked on its wooden hinges. Jobel stood just outside, listening.

Diamond Gulch was as quiet as it ever got. Wheelbarrows *creaked* as Chinese hauled gravel to the head box of a sluice. Hurdy-gurdy music made a mixed-up, discordant sound desecrating the chill, pine-fragrant air. Satisfied that no one was coming, Jobel hitched his twin pistols higher around his waist and walked down the path. John followed and saw him disappear through the rear door of the Territorial Hotel.

John entered half a minute later, finding a deserted hall lighted by a candle. At his left, rough-plank stairs led to the second floor. He could hear voices and the click of chips and traced the sounds to the front bar where the more affluent members of Diamond Gulch's society were drinking and bucking house games. Jobel was not there.

He retraced his steps. A Chinese lad in floppy, sky-blue

pants and shirt came downstairs, carrying a tray.

"Field Mecklin's room," John said, tossing a small nugget in the tray.

"Seventeen!" cried the happy Chinese.

Seventeen was at the head of the stairs, door closed. He listened, hearing first Field Mecklin's voice, then Jobel's. He was unable to distinguish more than a word or two, but it made no difference. He was sure of Jobel.

Nights were not long in Montana Territory during the summer season, and dawn was already on its way. A man named McCabe was sitting guard at the stage office.

"Oh, you," he yawned, putting aside his gun. "You're lookin' for Enfield? He went some place. Last Chance, maybe."

John went outside. He sat in front, watching dawn grow up, silhouetting the jagged mountain horizon. It was less than an hour before the departure of the Benton coach with its ten thousand dollar load of gold. He wished he was certain what Mecklin would do.

John rose with sudden decision, strode to the parson's, and out again through the back door with a blanket rolled under his arm. The Mexican hostler was asleep as usual, so John caught the pony. He rode, skirting the mountain, and cut back to town, reaching the Benton road where it made a short, steep pitch from the gulch bottom.

It was a spot few observers would consider a likely one for a hold-up, but after riding shotgun on the route John knew what he was about. He worked rapidly, making slits through the blanket for head and wrists, slipping it on, tying a bandanna across his face. About his middle, and outside the blanket, he cinched his Navy Colts. He looked squat and grotesque.

Innumerable trunks of slim lodgepole pine had been

cleared and tossed in piles beside the road. He dragged one out, broke off its small branches, and laid it across the road, just above the crest of the steep rise. Then he waited, bandanna lifted, chewing tobacco.

VII

The sun was rising, sending hot beams over the slim evergreens. It was time for the coach. At last he heard it—a *jingle* of harness chains, *crunch* of iron-tired wheels. He lowered the bandanna and hid, squatting in rose briar, the butt of the lodgepole in one hand.

Hoofs made a *clip-clopping* right below. The horses slowed, having trouble with footing and heavy coach. He waited until the heads of the lead team appeared, then he rose, lifting the lodgepole trunk, propping it high on rose thorns.

From his downhill position the driver was unable immediately to see what was wrong. His team had merely stopped and swung to the right, wading up to their shoulders in brush.

"You dirty, putrefied Injun bait!" he was bellowing, rolling out his long whip.

John stood up, a Navy in each hand. He was about level with the driver and guard in their high seat.

"Put on the brake," John said, disguising his voice.

The guard stared at him, jaw sagging, shotgun between his knees muzzle up. John's thumbs racked back the hammers. That sent the driver into action. He seized the hand brake, drawing it.

"Thar," said John. "Just keep your hands like that and you won't get in a bit of trouble. Now drop the shotgun overboard." He waited until it fell to the ground. "Give him the reins, driver."

The driver obeyed.

"Thar's a treasure chest in the for'ard boot. Toss her down."

The driver dragged out the heavy metal box and dumped it overboard.

"You gents have been most co-operative," John said, dropping the lodgepole trunk. "Now get movin'. Fast. And don't stop too quick."

He watched the coach lunge up the grade and disappear behind galloping horses. Moving quickly, then, he tossed away his blanket, and carried the chest uphill where Patches waited. He had originally intended merely to haul the treasure box back to the stage station, but its cumbersome weight made him change his mind. It would be easier to dump the bullion in a saddlebag.

He aimed at the lock, reconsidered. It would be too bad to ruin a box worth twenty to thirty dollars. He went to work with his sheath knife, finally succeeding in jimmying open the locks. He lifted the cover. Gunnysack had been placed around the contents. He lifted the sack and stood back with a surprised movement. It contained bullet lead, tinned powder, and box after box of percussion caps. A bullet from his Navy would have blasted him to kingdom come.

He chuckled. Enfield was smart, all right. He'd handed out his secret to all those who had an opportunity of being Mecklin spies, telling about the shipment of Benton gold, and he'd set this trap to blast the guilty one's head off.

Patches had his head up, jingling bit chains. John could hear nothing. The spruce and pine forest pressed closely around him cutting off his view.

A twig snapped. He spun around, Navy drawn. A voice

cut the forest stillness.

"Surrounded, road agent! If you'd rather have a bullet than a rope, just make your play."

There were other voices—the kind made by men moving through forest cover.

He opened his fingers, letting the Navy fall.

"Now, that was sensible," the voice said. "Unbuckle the other one and save yourself from temptation." John did as he was told. "Now maybe you'd better get your hands up. You're a ring-tailed catamount once you get to war pathin', and I think we'll play her safe."

A huge, blunt-faced man came in sight, a long-barreled Texas Derringer in each hand. They were smooth bores, probably loaded with enough buckshot to stop a charge of cavalry. The man was Buffalo Browers, captain of the Diamond Gulch vigilance committee.

Other men followed him, armed men with determined faces. One was tall, handsome Field Mecklin. There was an expression of smug satisfaction on the turned-down corners of his mouth.

A skinny little fellow with a rusty face and albino-pale eyes peered at John from a couple of angles and nodded importantly. "That's him, all right. That's the old Comanche himself. I seen him at Horse Prairie, and I'd know him anywheres."

"Of course, he's Comanche John," Mecklin said quietly.

"I'm John Jones, a Christian gentleman. Ask the parson at. . . ."

"We should hang that fake preacher, too," Mecklin sneered.

"What am I accused of?" John demanded, turning to Browers.

Browers looked shocked, then decided to laugh. "What

are you accused of! Stand thar by that open treasure chest just took off a robbed coach and ask what's he accused of. Now that takes a check for you."

"This is Enfield property, ain't it?"

"Reckon it is."

"Then you better bring Jack Enfield around, and as. . . ."

"You danged idiot, who do you think told us the coach was goin' to get robbed? Who do you think sent us out here if not Jack Enfield?"

"Anyhow, I want a trial. It's every man's privilege to. . . ."

"You've had your trial a couple of times already, I reckon, and now you're goin' to get the hangin' you was sentenced to." He looked around. "You brung us to a good spot, I'll say that for ye, John. Thar seems to be no special shortage of trees."

Someone tossed out a coil of windlass rope. It struck the earth near John's boots, and for a few seconds the men stared at it. The albino picked it up and commenced wrapping a big, clumsy hangman's knot.

John chewed, took aim, and plastered a white quartz pebble with tobacco juice. "All right, I'm Comanche John. I admit it. I know when I'm licked. We're down to the case cyards and you've coppered my last bet. Them as lives offen stagecoaches will die with a hemp halter around his windpipe, as the Good Book says. Reckon I was lucky that the vigilantes in Bannack and Lewiston, and down in Californy weren't as sharp as this 'n' or I'd have been hung a good bit ago."

Buffalo Browers chuckled, enjoying the flattery. "You're the cool one, sure enough."

"Yep, I been havin' the time o' my life robbin' coaches lately. Two of 'em betwixt hyar and Last Chance. One on her way to Virginny City. Two of 'em between Diamond Gulch and Benton. I sure got a stack o' dust hid away, and I'm mournful not to get the chance of spendin' it." He singled out Wilks Iverson of the W & I Mercantile. "Too bad for you, too, Iverson, because a couple o' them gold pokes had your brand."

Iverson elbowed forward. He was young with a pair of eyes that made him seem old. "Where is it?"

"Ho, ho!" roared Comanche John, stamping and beating the legs of his homespun pants. "Wants to know whar I hid it. Hangin' me, and now he wants favors. Why would I be tellin' *you* whar I hid it?"

The albino runt had tossed the rope over a gnarled limb, but Iverson held up one hand. "Let's not be in too big a hurry here. Of course, he's got gold from those coaches. He hasn't been gambling it away, so he still has it. All that gold." His eyes looked wistful.

Until that moment Field Mecklin had been keeping in the background. Now he strode forward. "He has a gang out here in the hills. He's only stalling to give them a chance to stage a rescue."

"We'll take care of the gang, if he has one, I reckon," said Buffalo Browers. "Nothin' I'd like more than to get a crack at eight or ten o' them dirty road agents. I only wish I had every road agent in the territory here. By hunkies, we'd put on a dance, and a damned light-footed one, too."

"Get the rope ready!" said Mecklin. His voice was not especially loud, but it had a saw-toothed edge of command. "Bring his pony over. We'll use it for the drop."

Men started obeying, even lumbering, obstinate Browers, but not Iverson. Iverson was not large, but he was no coward. He faced Mecklin. "There's a lot more than principle involved in this as far as I'm concerned. There's some of my gold, and, if there's a chance of getting it back, I want it."

"He's lying to you. He hasn't hidden any gold."

John guffawed. "How do you know, Mecklin?"

Mecklin's face had turned grayish beneath his tan. He knew everyone was looking at him. He had no answer for the obvious insinuation in John's question. He drew a single, deep breath, struggling to keep back his rage. Then without warning he set his heels and swung a right-hand blow to John's unprotected jaw.

John went down as though struck by a club. Mecklin would have leaped in and trampled his face as he had Jack Enfield's, but Browers stopped him. "Here, now. I know how you feel about the varmint, but just the same that ain't the way a vigilance member should act."

John came to his knees, blood from mashed lips staining his whiskers. "You're a brave man, Mecklin," he said with mock admiration.

Iverson asked: "Where'd you hide that dust?"

John considered while he stood up. He kept wiping blood with the back of his hand. "Tell ye what . . . I'll make it a sportin' proposition, seein' I'm a gentleman o' the South whar such things are in considerable favor. I'll lead you to the gold on one provision . . . to wit, put me on Patches, my hoss, and give me a fifty-yard runnin' start. Then, if you catch me, I'll get hung without complaint."

There was a mutter of objection. No one except Iverson and a couple more who were financial losers showed much enthusiasm.

"Get the horse over here!" Mecklin barked.

"What's wrong with givin' him a dog's chance?" demanded Iverson. "*If* he can produce the gold."

The vigilantes seemed to be hanging in the balance.

"Make it a forty-yard start," drawled John. "Or are you boys hyar in Diamond Gulch too yaller-gutted to make a gamble?"

"Ah, hell, gamble with him," said a miner. "He couldn't get away on that Injun cayuse."

"Where'd you hide it?" asked Browers.

"At that old White Gulch drift mine that Bogey opened when he was prospectin' out of Montana City three, four year ago."

"Why, that's seven mile."

"I wish I could move it closer for your convenience," mourned John, "but if you want your heavy color back, I guess we'll have to ride all seven miles of her."

VIII

The cavalcade skirted the town, passing close to the big new houses of Iverson and Gerstenhover, and headed up the mountain on the old trail to White Gulch.

The placers of White Gulch were considerably older than those at Last Chance or Diamond Gulch, having been worked chiefly in the late 'Fifties by miners from Gold Creek. Comanche John had not visited White Gulch for two years, but he could see that the tunnels to Bogey's abandoned drift mine were still open. Approaching closer, other things were visible—the ore chute coming steeply down the hill from an upper bench, the air shaft still farther, looking like a truncated chimney with the log cribbing built around it, the ore bin, and the cabin with brush growing in front of its door.

He tried to remember the details of the mine's interior. The lower tunnel followed bedrock for about four hundred feet. Midway along it was a shaft through shale that explored a prehistoric gulch bed. A drift had been dug along this lower level connecting with the air shaft, where, if things worked out right, John might have a chance to escape. In case of cave-ins, of course, he would be trapped, but then he'd been trapped on yonder hillside, too.

The horses splashed across shallow White Creek, Iverson, John, and Browers in the lead, the albino just behind with a sawed-off across the pommel, and the rest stringing out in twos and threes.

John drew up beside the ore bin. "Beggin' your permission, gents, can I get down?"

"Git, but don't try anything jumpy."

Iverson sat still a while, looking around and speaking in a dry, suspicious voice. "Seems that you traveled a long way to hide that stuff."

"Yep," John answered cheerfully, tying Patches.

They climbed the short slope to the tunnel. They stopped at the portal.

"Candle?" asked Buffalo Browers.

John found one stuck in a niche of the wall, and Iverson lighted it with a patent sulphur match. There was barely room for two abreast in the narrow tunnel.

"How far?" Iverson asked, going ahead with the candle.

"Far enough."

Iverson moved slowly, stepping over gravel and sand that had caved between the timbers of the walls. Behind him was Comanche John and Browers, holding his arm, then the albino with the sawed-off, and most of the others.

The tunnel made a bend. Light no longer reached them from outside. After thirty or forty steps the tunnel curved again. There would be a third curve, this one almost at right angles, and a few steps beyond that the mouth of the shaft. It was farther than John had expected. Iverson stopped just short of the last turn. He held his candle forward, letting its light fall on an undisturbed heap of sand and gravel that had sifted down covering a section of wooden track.

"When were you in here last?"

"Two, three days ago." John chewed. "Just after robbin' that Last Chance stagecoach."

"Through *here?*" Iverson pointed at the undisturbed sand.

"Yep."

"I haven't seen a track."

"Of course not!" cried Mecklin, trying to crowd forward around men who almost filled the narrow passage. "He's never been here before. Let's get out of this damned hole and do the job we started to do."

John said: "Iverson, you don't see a sign o' my boots because I didn't want ye should. Think I aimed to be tracked in here? If you'd like, I'll show ye the Injun system I use."

Nobody spoke for a second, so John crowded forward. For the moment Buffalo Browers was placed before the albino's sawed-off. "Leggo my arm!" John said to Browers.

Browers released him, thought better of it, grabbed again.

"Stop that man!" screamed Mecklin.

Iverson had not expected him to be so close. He turned around, drawing the Navy he carried in the holster at his waist. The candle was close, and it was a simple matter to blow it out. The blackness of the mine was sudden and complete—a blackness filled with shouting, stamping men. Buffalo Browers still held John's arm, but John was unexpectedly strong. He doubled over, spinning, whipping himself free.

He felt Iverson's gun ramming his belly. He seized the barrel and twisted it down. The gun exploded, driving lead and burning powder to the floor. The close space was filled with strangling powder smoke. He ripped the gun free, flinging Iverson back along the tunnel. Someone grunted when he hit.

John backed away, one hand on the wall. He reached the bend and went on. Shouting voices rebounded, mingling in a nightmarish babble. A light came on, making a wavering, yellow reflection around the bend. Just ahead of him John could see some poles laid close together, forming a bridge over the shaft. He pulled the poles apart, lowering himself. Below him, the shaft was a well of darkness. He swung free of the side—dropped. It was deeper than he expected. For a sickening moment he seemed to be falling through limitless space. Then he struck and fell back, up to his ankles and one wrist in muck.

He stood and felt around for the drift. The voices were close above. Candle flame revealed a man's arm thrust down the shaft. Brightness of the light hid the face beyond.

"Can't see a damned thing," said Iverson's voice.

John moved out of sight along the mucky drift. It was poorly timbered. In some places, gravel had fallen, half filling it, but he could tell by the air that there was circulation, so the workings must still be open.

He reached the end of the drift, fumbling for the ladder. The ladder was a crude affair—pegs driven through single lengths of lodgepole. Far above was a tiny square of light.

He climbed slowly, making sure of each rickety rung. Two or three minutes passed. His nostrils caught a hint of pine fragrance from above. Voices babbled, apparently from many directions. The candle came in view—a pinpoint of light ninety feet below. Its rays, quickly eaten up by the dark air-shaft walls, did not reach him.

The shaft's mouth was only a dozen rungs above, but to reach it he would have to silhouette himself for a deadly three or four seconds. He paused, clung with his legs, and heaved back and forth on one of the timbers, springing it loose. It started a shower of gravel. The timber fell, tearing splinters, starting a larger roar of gravel.

A gun exploded amid alarmed voices. John clambered the

last rungs, seized the top of the cribbing, drawing himself over the top. He was outside with the sun shining down and the broad, spottily timbered mountain before him.

Someone shot, and the bullet lifted a pebble that struck his homespun pants. Three or four men had been posted at the portal. He dodged to cover as a second bullet whipped past.

He could make a dash for it up the mountain, but afoot he would be run down in ten minutes. For the moment he was safe behind the shaft cribbing. He bellied across to the upper tunnel dump. Four men revealed themselves at brief intervals below, fanning out, trying to pin him down until the others got outside.

John skirted the dump, crouching for a moment behind the criss-cross timber supports of the ore chute. Below he could see the chute terminating in the partly filled bin. A seedling pine grew at his feet. He tore it up by the roots. He swung over the edge of the ore chute, placing the pine beneath the seat of his pants. The chute was wood, polished by gravel until it had an oily brightness. With slippery, long pine needles under him, he was on his way with a speed that blurred the mountain and sucked breath from his lungs. Guns were *whanging* on both sides, but he had no impression of bullets.

The ore bin was two-thirds full of gravel. He hit it rolling. His head rammed the front, stunning him for an instant, but the logs gave a moment of protection. He steadied himself, swinging over the edge. Many shouting voices issued behind him, from the direction of the tunnel, but he could see no one. Patches was below. He dropped to the pony's back, jerked the hackamore free, headed downhill, through the creek with lead whipping like hornets in the air.

He swung from sight, following the old trail toward White City. The trail wound through heaps of washed gravel. It was a good trail—a trail that would take a man to Last Chance, or Eldorado, or a hundred other places, all of them distant from Diamond Gulch. In the midst of thick timber he left the trail and swung back, up and over a rocky bank, through brush, up a slowly steepening mountainside. Running hoofs approached along the trail, and then grew distant. The last thing those vigilantes would expect was his return to Diamond Gulch.

"Yep," he grunted, at long last getting a chance to freshen his chew of tobacco. "That just shows how damn' little they know of the ways o' Comanche John!"

IX

Comanche John reached the divide and breathed his pony for a while, looking back across White Gulch. There was no sign of life in that direction. Ahead of him he could see the roofs of Diamond Gulch, their bleached shakes reflecting the bright, mid-morning sun. The air of mountain summer was clear and dustless, rarified, undistorted by heat wave or humidity. He could see the town in minute detail, almost as though he were there, except that things were made small by distance. A coach drawn by six horses was rolling down the road from town.

He cursed, and his sudden movement in the saddle made the Nez Percé pony start downhill at a stiff-legged canter. The coach was headed for Benton, and there'd be gold on it this time—that ten-thousand-dollar insured shipment, and Max Jobel would be riding shotgun. *Yep, you're a smart lad, Jack Enfield,* he mused, letting the pony's motion bump words in his mind, *but you're tryin' mighty hard to out-figger yourself this time.*

The slope flattened out with the trail moving straight across a park where deer grazed. A girl, riding side-saddle, galloped toward him on a big, chestnut horse. It was Bess McGrail. The chestnut was unused to a woman's riding style, and kept turning around, tossing his head nervously as she reined him in.

"Thank the Lord it's you!" she said.

"You wanted me?"

"I saw them. Those . . . vigilantes. I thought they intended to hang you. I was riding to stop them. I found out from Mister Gerstenhover. . . ."

"I ain't got time now, little gal. There's a coach leavin' town that I think would be a prime idee to stop. She's got gold on her, and them dry-gulchers o' Mecklin's are probably fixin' to take it." He peered at her. "Maybe you don't believe that about your future husband?"

She simply stared at him.

He said: "You can't fool me, gal. You don't care a hoot for that brassy dandy. It's Jack Enfield you're fixin' to care about." Her eyes did not deny it. "You better wheel around and ride back. Get to Enfield as quick as you can. Tell him what Gerstenhover said . . . whatever it was. And tell him the chances are I'll need a little follow-up backin' on that coach, if he cares to take a ride."

It was a mile to town. He hit the gulch street traveling on a dead run. The pony was tiring. He drew up in front of the W & I Mercantile. Three saddle horses were tied at the rack. He chose a big-chested gray, jerked the reins free, mounted. A man ran out, cursing him, but John had already lashed the horse to a gallop and did not look back.

The gray was faster than he expected. He soon proved to have a heavy-legged endurance, too. For three miles the road wound along the bottoms, crossing and re-crossing Diamond

Creek. He caught sight of the coach rolling ahead. Dust from its wheels settled in a silver film through bright sunshine.

Far back, from the direction of town, riders were coming. He could not tell who they were. The road climbed a hillside making a series of looping turns. At one side was a saddle trail cutting steeply through timber. He saw the chance of intercepting the coach as it reached the crest. Little of that steep trail was required to take the gallop out of the bay, but he went on bravely, faster than a man could climb.

The hilltop was covered with bare rock and stunted juniper. John swung down. He could hear the coach and horses. The lead team was just coming into view. Long Lash and Jobel rocked in the high seat. There were no passengers.

John paused on the edge of a dug-out bank, partly hidden by a juniper. Jobel saw him just as he leaped. A reflex brought the shotgun around. It boomed, sending shot so close it nicked the sleeve of John's buckskin shirt. The blast frightened the horses, and they were away at a gallop. John caught the railing that circled the hurricane, hung with one hand, the Navy in the other. Jobel flung himself back, one elbow resting on the jolting top, trying to get the shotgun barrel beyond Long Lash for a second shot. The Navy hammered, its heavy slug slamming Jobel backward.

Jobel made a last grab. He stood, shotgun gone and fingers tearing his chest. He fell backward with a lurch of the coach, struck ground, and flopped over, laying huddled at the road's edge. Long Lash was trying to get at his gun.

"Don't do it!" barked John.

"Ye damned Yankee!" the driver shouted, naming John the lowest thing he could think of. "Ye damned Yankee spy."

"I ain't, and I ain't got time to explain. Your spy's back thar on the ground, and I can prove it."

"All right, you got the drop." Long Lash was easing back

on the ribbons, slowing his galloping team.

"Keep going!" John shouted.

His eyes had caught a single flash of gun shine. It was less than fifty yards ahead where the road curved around another dug-out bank. It was an ambush with no time to turn back. John jerked the whip from the driver's hand and laid it over the backs of the horses, setting them out on the dead run.

"What the devil . . . !"

They swung at the curve. A log had been placed across the road. On each side crouched a masked man—one with a shotgun, the other with two Navies.

"That answer your question?" bellowed John.

Even if they'd wanted, there'd have been no time to stop. The road agent on the right swung up his shotgun, shouting something that could not be heard over the thunder of the rolling coach. The Navy pounded in John's hand, driving the man to earth. The other road agent was diving for cover, seeing at the last terrified moment that he was being pinned between stagecoach and bank.

John was standing, bellowing: "Hunt your holes, ye belly-crawlin' blow snakes, I'm a ring-tailed roarer, and I got a handful of sudden death!"

Miraculously all six of the horses cleared the obstruction, but the coach's front wheels struck with ruinous force. One of them splintered, letting the coach bend sidewise over slivered spokes. The coach drove its side into the bank, hanging on one rear wheel, the front hub digging a deep furrow. The six horses dragged it on. It went over on its side and at last came to a grinding stop, obscured by a roll of dust.

The dust was lazy about settling. It parted slowly revealing Long Lash, face down, arms outflung. He might have been dead for all the movement he made.

John started to stand. He was hit by a bushwhack bullet

and turned half around. He went to his knees behind the coach. He steadied himself, recovering from bullet shock. He still had the Navy. He could hear the bushwhacker's jeering laugh—Blackie Andros. Blackie thought the bullet had killed him, but he stayed down for a cautious moment. John edged the side of his face into view. He glimpsed Blackie among slide rock above the bank. Blackie leaped back, firing. John's Navy roared the same instant.

Blackie was hit. He still tried to crawl. He staggered to his feet, gun gone, arms clutching his chest. He turned slowly and fell face forward, skidding and flopping loosely before coming to a stop on the steep hill.

John tore his buckskin shirt open for a look at his own wound. The bullet had struck ribs on the left side and glanced around. It was bleeding, but not too badly.

A clatter of hoofs sounded, and a horse came to a sliding stop. Field Mecklin sat tall and erect on his winded bay horse, staring at the smashed coach. His eyes swung up the hillside. Apparently he couldn't figure it out.

"There're runnin', Mecklin."

Comanche John was up and walking toward him along the rocky road, Navy thrust in the band of his homespuns. Mecklin watched him, a light twitch of fear showing in his eyes. He turned a little. His left hand clutched bridle reins until their knuckles were bloodless. He kept wetting his dry lips.

John said: "Why don't ye run with your bushwhackers, Mecklin?"

"I don't run from swine!" he answered, trying to bring the old-time sneer to his lips.

Mecklin's pistol was out, but he had to level it over the horse's neck. John's Navy exploded, its bullet tearing the ivory-handled S & W from Mecklin's hand.

"Draw your other one," John drawled. "I'd like to fix ye up so's your Chinee servant would have to feed you until time for the hangin'."

But Mecklin didn't try for the other gun. The bullet had gone between gun and hand and then followed the bone to his elbow. He hung for a moment, weaving, clutching his forearm. He fell to the ground, remained, half sitting, one leg doubled under him.

Other riders approached, Jack Enfield, and behind him a shotgun guard from Virginia City, and next the girl.

"Gold's safe," John grunted. "I was only tryin' to save it from these lads this mornin' when I stopped that decoy coach. I don't know how the gal found out, but I suppose she told you."

"Yes, I know. Gerstenhover told her how things were. He's a good Dutchman." He talked, never taking his eyes from Mecklin. "Who was the spy . . . Jobel?"

"Yes, Jobel."

John climbed the hillside and caught the gray horse. Much as he liked Patches, the gray seemed to be a better traveler. Anyhow, there were certain vigilantes down Bannack way who were on the watch for that pinto horse. "I got me some wages comin', I reckon. You can pay it to the kind owner o' this gray horse, and thank him for his thoughtfulness in leavin' him handy for me. The parson will take Patches. If you'd like, you can toss my belts and Navies on the Eldorado coach. Ask Buffalo Browers for 'em."

"You're not leaving . . . ?"

"Yep, son. I reckon it's for the best all around. I saved Mecklin for you, thinkin' maybe you're like to have him testify to a few things before he got hung. That's a hangin' I'd like to attend, too, only I'm afraid Buffalo would see me and hanker to make it a double one."

John sat on his horse for a while, looking at the young man and the girl. A finer couple he'd never seen. "Wish you'd take her hand in yourn," he said to Enfield.

"Like this?"

"Yep. I want my last look just like that. Now, that's a picture for a man to take down the long trail with him."

He nudged the gray and headed him up the mountain trail. He disappeared in timber, but his voice floated down, singing creakily in rhythm with the *clip-clop* of the horse's hoofs.

Comanche John rode to Fino Gulch
With a wild and rowdy crew,
With his old pal Whisky Anderson
And that varmint, Henry Drew.

That Varmint, Comanche John

I

After a long climb, the stagecoach reached the summit of Birdtail Pass. It was sunset there, on the ridge of the world, with the vast panorama of mountain Montana spread out below. The black-whiskered man who had found a seat between the driver and the shotgun guard took a long, narrow look at it, leaned back to shoot tobacco juice across the hurricane, and, wiping his lips on the back of his hand, commented: "Road-agent country."

He was rather short and close-coupled. His age might have been anywhere between thirty-five and fifty—it was hard to tell through his unkempt tangle of whiskers. On his head was a shapeless black slouch hat. His dusty homespun pants were thrust in the tops of dusty jackboots. Over his faded linsey shirt he wore a Nez Percé buckskin vest with most of the beadwork gone. It was a garb typical enough in that gold rush year of 1864, except for the two Navy Colts he wore in worn holsters on crossed belts. They made him a little special.

The coach rolled easily through scrub timber, then with a sudden pitch it started down, and there was a grind of leather brake shoes. The driver, a tall, reddish and long-mustached man who went by the name of Whooper Owens, answered: "Road agents be damned. These Nor'western highwaymen!

In my estimate they don't stack up any too well ag'in' the kind we had back in Californy."

The black-whiskered man showed new interest. "Waal, now!"

"Mind ye, I'm not the type that brags, but you're looking at a man that was robbed by Comanche John!"

"Comanche John? Can't say I ever heered of him."

"Never heered of him! Holy saints and bald-headed hell!" Owens leaned forward to see past the black-whiskered man and address the shotgun guard. "Hey, Rambo . . . did ye give an ear to that? Here's a man that never heered tell of Comanche John!"

Rambo showed his ill temper by something he muttered from one side of his bulldog mouth and kept watch on the steeply winding road. The coach, heavily laden with express and passengers, was barely moving, and it would be an easy target from the bank that rose vertically to the right. The sawed-off shotgun that had rested in the scabbard boot between his feet he now freed and held in both hands.

"Co-man-che?" the black-whiskered man repeated. "Like the Injuns?"

"Yes," the driver said, "but he's not an Injun. Hailed from Pike County, just like me. The ridin'est, shootin'est, whoopin'est sidewinder that ever put bullet lead through an Abolitionist, that's what he is."

The guard said: "He get in front of my gun and I reckon he'd fill the same six-by-three as anybody else."

"Ye wouldn't have the chance," the driver objected. "The old Comanche would stand at the turn of the trail, yonder, and shoot the tobacky right out of your mouth. Let me tell ye about the time he took me for a coach load of the heavy color when I was driving between Chinyman's Bar and Fethar River. It was nigh dark, later than this, and I had no less than *three* shotgun guards along, when this black-whiskered varmint. . . ." He chuckled and said: "Stranger, you don't need to be proud of the underbrush on *your* face, because compared to the old Comanche you're as clean-cheeked as the rear of a newborn babe, and that's a fact. Waal, as I was saying. . . ."

"I heard that story too damned many times already," Rambo said.

"Worry ye some?" the stranger asked.

"I ain't a bit worried." He slapped the shotgun. "Anybody git in front of old Agnes here, and I'll chop 'em up like buffaler in a Blackfoot stew."

The driver thereupon pulled his collar to loosen it and lifted his magpie voice in a song.

Oh, gather 'round, ye teamster men
And listen to my tale
Of the worst sidewindin' varmint
That rides the outlaw trail,
He wears the name Comanche John
And he comes from Old Missou,
Where many a Concord coach he stopped
And many a gun he drew.
He first rode down to Yuba Town
In the good year 'Sixty-Two,
With a pal named Whisky Anderson
And one named Henry Drew.
They robbed the bank at Forty-Rod,
They stopped the western mail,
And many a cheek did blanch to hear
Their names spoke' on the trail.
But Whisky was a drinkin' man
And Henry was the same
And ere the year had come and gone. . . .

Rambo broke in: "Will you stop that infernal racket? A man has to use his ears as well as his eyes in my business."

The black-whiskered man said: "I wouldn't think there'd be much danger of *this* coach being robbed."

Rambo bellowed from close range. "Why not?"

"Waal, if I was a road agent, or such varmint, instead of a man of high religious principles that spent a whole winter shacked up with a preacher, I'd pick on a coach rolling *from* Last Chance rather than *toward* her." He kicked the express box and mail sack that lay beneath their feet. "Whar was that sealed? In Salt Lake? No gold thar. Few watches, maybe. Greenbacks. Worthless Union paper. They'll be usin' it to wad guns with one of these days when old Robbie Lee takes Washington."

"I don't like that sort of talk ag'in' the gov'ment."

"This is the wild Nor'west, whar a man can choose any side he wants to."

"And it seems to me you're a mite well up on road agentin' for somebody that never heered tell of Comanche John."

It was close quarters on the seat, and the black-whiskered man moved to shift his twin Navies to a more comfortable position. "Waal, now that I gave ear to that song, it seems I *have* heered of Comanche John, after all. Calling him a common road agent was what mixed me up, because from what I been told he's a man of noble instincts that takes from the rich and gives to the pore, and never stops a coach unless it's so loaded down with the heavy yaller as to be downright cruel to the horses. Share and share alike, that's Comanche John's motto."

"He's a low-down, killing, thieving varmint, and anyhow the vigilantes hung him over in Boise City," the guard put in.

Whooper Owens said: "They hung him in Nevada, and Rocky Bar, and in Yaller Jacket, too. Every time they stiffen a rope with some poor, flea-bit, two-shilling sluice robber, they brag that they hung Comanche John. He's not in I-dee-ho. He's still in Californy."

The sun had set, and darkness closed in rapidly as the road dropped through tall timber. It followed a steep gulch bottom where a tiny stream raced among granite boulders. Side channels swelled the volume of the stream, the V of the gulch broadened, and the coach, slowing against the hand brake, turned and creaked in a top-heavy manner across a ford bowered by huge spruce trees.

With the hind wheels still in the water, the lead team lunged and came to a stop, shoulder-deep in underbrush at one side of the road. Owens was up and cursing. He *gee-hawed,* both hands filled with reins. Rambo, after being momentarily knocked off balance, held to the seat, and started around with his double shotgun, but a voice from beside the road stopped him with a shrill: "Hands up!"

The swing team was over the rumps of the leaders. Owens got the wheelers to back a trifle and saved a tangled harness. A passenger had his head thrust out, shouting questions. It was all mix-up and excitement.

A slim, slight figure garbed in black and masked in black appeared from the dense underbrush with a double-barreled pistol in each hand. The pistols were fine pieces, bright with silver, but old-timers, Ten-Gauge, smooth bore. Both hammers of both pistols were cocked, and the hands that gripped them were very tense. The black-whiskered man slid down on bent knees, trying to get the more vital parts of his body out of the way.

"Sit up, or I'll kill you!" The words had a brassy ring. The voice was obviously disguised. Evening light, shining on the engraved, silvery sides of the barrels, made rapid, trembly glimmers. "I'm not alone. If you think I am, try something."

Owens said: "Damn it, nobody's. . . ."

"Toss down the mail sack."

"How in hell can I . . . ?"

"You!" addressing the whiskered man. "Get the mail. Drop it down here."

The shotgun guard said: "I'll git it!"

He was on the edge of the seat, the double shotgun held between his knees. He took hold of the barrel. He laid it down, butt toward the road agent. He did it very slowly with his right hand while his left slipped beneath his jacket. His elbow, out of view, rammed the black-whiskered man in the ribs. He had slipped a small, side-hammer Colt from his belt. He aimed it across his waist as he came up with the mail sack. It exploded, lashing powder flame through the shadowed darkness, but at the final instant the black-whiskered man had nudged his elbow, throwing his aim off.

The horses, frightened, were off at a lunge. Both the road agent's guns exploded. The black-whiskered man, dragging Rambo and helped by the jerk of the coach, saved both of them from the full blast of buckshot.

He clung to the top rail as the coach careened up the bank, thudded over the ten-inch log that had been placed there as a check, and raced along a winding road through the baffling light and shadow of timber.

Owens, now on his feet, swung his long lash, urging the horses to even greater speed. Rambo was hit. He was writhing and cursing, one leg over the side of the hurricane deck. The black-whiskered man held him, but he was heavy, and each leap of the coach took him another inch or so over the edge. "Slow down, damn ye!" he shouted. "Slow down, or I'll lose your shotgun guard."

Owens bellowed back: "What can a man do with six Injun mules?"

After a quarter mile he got the fright and lather out of them, and slowed the coach to a gentle perambulation. No sign of pursuit. He kept watch while the whiskered man got Rambo full length on the top of the coach.

Rambo had now recovered from bullet shock and was able to fight back. "Let me up, you dirty Rebel. You were in with 'em."

"In with 'em! I saved your hide!"

"You rammed my arm or I'd o' had him right between the eyes."

"Here, now. You stay put. You tooken a couple of buckshot, and you're leaking all over my new buckskin vest. Typical Yankee gratitude if I ever seen it. Now lie whilst I patch you up so maybe we can deliver ye to the sawbones instead of the undertaker when we git to Last Chance."

Rambo writhed and dug his boot heels in the coach top while the black-whiskered man dug out the buckshot with his Bowie. Afterward he tore a large bandanna into strips, plastered the arm and shoulder wounds with chewing tobacco, and bound them tightly.

An hour later, with timber and mountains behind and the lights of Last Chance twinkling ahead of them, Rambo was able to sit up and ask for whisky. He took a big one from Owens's emergency bottle, slapped the cork back, and said huskily: "Anyhow, we saved the mail sack."

The black-whiskered man said: "Ye better look again."

"What?"

"I say ye better look again. The mail sack's gone."

"Whar is it?"

"That's something I was going to ask you. I ain't seen it since we forded the crick."

The express strongbox was beneath their feet, but the mail sack had, indeed, disappeared. Grinning, placidly chewing his tobacco, the whiskered man moved back and hunkered on the hurricane while making room for Rambo's frenzied search.

They crossed a rocky flat. A bridge made a hollow sound under the wheels. On both sides were long drifts of gravel, the tailings from placer operations farther up the gulch. There were rubbish heaps and the flimsy shacks of Chinatown.

Unnoticed the black-whiskered man bellied over the rear of the coach. He hung by one hand, his boots dangling, while his other hand searched deeply in the rear boot. Then he dropped lightly to the road. The coach left him, and the night seemed very quiet.

"Share and share alike, that's my motto," he said.

With the mail sack on his shoulder he took a roundabout path toward the camp's main street.

II

Main Street wound along the bottom of the gulch, a group of buildings here and a group there separated by stretches of gravel still being worked for gold. He walked beneath a flume that dripped roily water. A shake pole and plank walk skirted a placer pit where Chinese labored by the light of pitch torches, carrying baskets of gravel to the head box of a sluice where a watchman sat in a tiny look-out shanty with a gun across his knees. Wagon roads zigzagged up the steep sides of the gulch to little clusters of cabins that clung to the higher benches and to hard-rock mines on the flanks of the mountains beyond.

The black-whiskered man followed one of the gulch side roads until the main part of town lay beneath him, then he stopped to give it a long scrutiny. There was no alarm in him, or curiosity. It had merely become his way of life to fix each new scene in mind, its individual parts, its entrances and its exits. The stage had drawn up beneath a pole awning, and there was considerable loud talk and dashing around. Doors slammed and boots thudded the walks. Fiddles and Spanish harps played music in polka time.

He descended, having located the two buildings that interested him most—the jail and a long log-and-clapboard building topped by a rude steeple. He went to the jail first, dropped the mail sack, stepped inside. A heavily booted, heavily armed man got his feet down from the desk and said: "If you come to tell me about that stage hold-up, all I got to say is this . . . my job is patrolling Last Chance, and. . . ."

"Now that's a sensible attitude. If they *never* get the one that made off with that gov'ment mail sack, it's all right with me. I'm a stranger hereabouts, just having arrived with a mind to going into business, and one of the things it's my policy to check on is the state of law and order. As one of the men who makes your job possible, would ye mind showing me your strongest cell?"

The man looked him up and down, grunted, laughed, whacked dust from his pants, and said: "There she is, first door to your right. Eighteen-inch ponderosa timbers, cross-ribbed and bolted, window bars of strap iron, strong enough to hold a circus elephant." When the whiskered man had his look and reappeared, he asked: "By the way, what's your line? Can't say you look exactly like a banker or a storekeeper or any of those things."

The whiskered man paused in the door and chewed the question over, his eyes narrow, his hands hanging by habit beneath the smooth-worn butts of his Navy Colts. "Why, it's not exactly good manners to ask a man's line of employment before he hangs his shingle up, but I'll tell ye this . . . in my business, I go along life's highway lightening the loads o' them pilgrims that carry more around than they should. Share and share alike is my motto."

He walked down the street, the mail sack rolled under his arm, until he stood by the steepled building where a board sign erected over the sidewalk read:

PALACE OF SALVATION
Rev. Jeremiah Parker

Beneath it was a banner, wind-whipped and rain-streaked:

Repent Ye or Ye'll Roast in Hell

The door stood open, but there was no light. He went inside.

"Parson, be ye thar?" he called. "Parson, your lost sheep has returned to the fold, hungry for grub and righteousness."

There was no answer. Enough light came from a saloon window across the way to reveal the main outlines of the room. It was long and low-ceilinged, filled with puncheon benches. A fancy-cut oak pulpit, probably hauled by ox team all the way from Salt Lake City, stood on a platform at the far end. The platform also accommodated a little hand-bellows organ and a case filled with books and tracts.

"Why, this is mighty fancy, might-ee fancy." He stopped at a door covered with gunnysack draperies that led to the parson's living quarters, and spoke again. "Parson, be ye thar?"

He lifted the drape and went in. He groped, banged his shins on the wood box, cursed, found a chair, tilted it against the wall, and, hat over his eyes, heels hooked in the rungs, thumbs hooked in his gun belts, he chewed and waited.

Music drifted on the clear mountain air, lulling him, and he dozed. An hour might have passed when suddenly he jerked erect to a sound of someone in the room out front.

He remained in his chair. He made no move. Two persons came through the door. One of them lifted the lid off the tiny prospector's cook stove and blew a coal to brightness. The glow revealed his face. He was gray and skinny with wild hair and huge eyes that could have belonged to an avenging prophet from the pages of the Old Testament. He got a splinter to blazing and lighted a candle with it. The flame, after long darkness, made the room seem very bright.

The second person was a girl, dressed in a brown riding skirt. She had changed from the black costume, but the black-whiskered man recognized her. It was she who had stopped the coach.

He sat still for a few seconds, chewing and grinning. Then he spat at the ash bucket and spoke: "Waal, Parson, here I be."

The parson spun on him, stiffened and pop-eyed from surprise. "Why, it's that varmint, Comanche John! Or be ye a ghost? I heard they'd strung you from a cottonwood in Boise City."

"No ghost, Parson. I got warmth in my body and flesh on my bones. Come here and feel of me if you like."

"*Yip-ee!* I told 'em so! I said they'd have to git up at thirteen o'clock in the morning to catch old Comanche John." Then he stiffened and glared. "What ye been up to? So help me, John, if ye been treadin' the paths of sin and highway robbery in spite of all the convertin' I've done on ye, I'll turn ye over to the law."

"Why, Parson, I'm as innocent as a babe unborn." He let his eyes travel to the girl. She had recognized him. She was small and pretty and frightened. "Besides, if I was in your position, I don't guess I'd shout too much about some other man being a highway robber. By the way, gal, you forgot this out at the foot of Birdtail Pass."

Very casually Comanche John picked up the mail sack. He appraised it from several angles, and tossed it to her. He said: "Parson, after this, when I give you a fine brace of double pistols, be good enough to smoke the bar'ls, or cover 'em with taller so they can't be identified. Why, that silver engraving stood out like a barber pole in San Francisco."

The parson cried: "Quit your grinning! There's no highway robbery about this!"

"Now you've took to seeing things my way. Share and share alike. . . ."

"No, it wasn't robbery. A mission of mercy, that's what. We have a good idea there's a letter in that sack that'd cost a man his life. When we get it, everything else in that bag will go where it belongs."

The girl tore the sack open with the parson's butcher knife. She dumped letters on the table and the floor. She searched with desperate excitement until she found the one she was looking for. With jumpy fingers she opened it.

"That it?" asked the parson.

"Oh, yes, thank God, it's it!"

"He names Mark?"

"Yes. Lieutenant Mark Clay."

Comanche John said: "Could I be so bold as to inquire. . . ." But no one listened to him. He waited until she was through scanning it in the light of the candle, and repeated: "Could *I* be so bold as ask what the thunder you're talking about?"

"This!" she said, handing it to him.

"Hmm. Damn, look at all them scratches. Thar's a great big one! Looks like a snake. Why, I know what that letter is!

That's an S, ain't it, Parson?"

The parson said—"It's a capital I."—and grabbed the letter away from him.

John asked: "Ye say that'd cost a man his life? What is it, an order from that low, ornery Abe Lincoln to send some poor, brave Confederate spy to the gallows?" The girl shot him a surprised glance, and he responded: "You mean I guessed it?"

The parson said: "It's not President Abraham Lincoln and the duly constituted authority of the realm that have *this* piece of killing in mind. It's the Rebels who want to carry their war and their slavery into this unspoiled land and set brothers to killing brothers. *That's* who it is."

"Ye mean that letter has something to do with the cause of the Southern Confederacy?"

"I mean it's some skullduggery thought up by Crews, that underground Knight of the Golden Circle outfit, who'd like to split the Nor'west off from the Union and jine with the Confederacy. Killing, that's what the Rebs have in mind . . . killing an officer of the Union Army that's here in civilian clothes, getting the deadwood on 'em. This letter would give him away, but it's *not being delivered!*"

Comanche John almost stopped chewing. His eyes had become narrow. "Waal, now. It's good to know I done something for the side o' righteousness."

"Yes, it *is* on the side o' righteousness to get at the truth of what's going on behind closed doors in that fancy, sinful London Hotel."

"A Union spy!"

"Savior of this country, if you want my estimate." He saw John start forward and cried to the girl: "Lyn! Don't let him get his hands on that letter."

But the whiskered man, moving with a swiftness unexpected in such a thickly coupled body, had pounced across the room. He grabbed it from her hand. He rammed it in a pocket of his homespuns. She tried to draw one of the double pistols that was thrust in the waist of her riding skirt, but with an upward swing of his hand he knocked it from her grasp.

At the door, with his right hand on the butt of a low-swinging Navy he faced them. "No, gal. It would grieve me to have to harm a hair of your head, but I will, and, Parson, that goes for you, because there's something bigger in this than friendship. This is the war, and all them brave lads dying at Pittsburgh Landing and Pea Ridge, the victims of Northern treachery. Parson, it grieves me to say this . . . we been through desert heat and squaw cookin' together, you lifted me from the black gulch of sin and regenerated me with the power of the Word in Nevady City and again in Baker Town, but this is the fork in the trail."

The girl cried: "Where are you going with that?"

"Why, I reckon I'll deliver it to the one it's addressed to."

The parson, his finger upraised on the end of a long arm until it almost touched the ceiling, cried: "Go ye from that door and I'll set the sheriff after ye, John. I will. I'll see you're hung to the highest tree in Last Chance."

"Now, Parson, that's thoughtful of ye. It is for a fact. When I get hung, I want a tall tree, a strong rope, and a good drop."

III

Comanche John paused at a saloon window to scrutinize the envelope. He looked at it from several angles. When a miner, plastered with muck from the placer pits, jostled past, he said: "Would you mind cipherin' this name and address for a man whose eddication never went so far as the three Rs?"

It was addressed to J. D. Crews, care of the London Hotel. He thrust it in his hip pocket and followed the miner's directions to the hotel, a large, ramshackle, three-story building perched on a shoulder of ground at a turn of the gulch. He took his time. His walk was a wary amble. He seemed careless and completely off guard, but his eyes, shaded by the brim of his black slouch hat, missed nothing along the busy street.

He stopped at the foot of some stairs leading to the London's shadowy front porch and freshened his chew of blackjack tobacco. Men, seated in the darkness, smoked and watched the steady *gee-haw* of freight outfits below. The lower floor of the hotel seemed to be divided into three roughly equal parts—a dining room on one side, a saloon and gaming room on the other, and the lobby in between.

He went inside the lobby. It was dimly lighted by amber-shaded oil lamps. It held the close odors of lamp smoke and furniture polish. He worked up his fresh chew, spotted a tall brass spittoon, and fired at it, chuckling with a marksman's satisfaction when he hit it dead center.

He walked to the desk and was about to ring the bell when a very fat and powerful man came through a door from an office and looked at him without favor.

"We take no teamsters here," he said.

With a slouch and a hitch of his shoulder, Comanche John unholstered his right-hand Navy. He spun it on his finger, examined the loads, and said: "I been some troubled with wax in my ears lately. Would you mind repeating what you just said?"

The fat man had a sick smile. He said: "You can have any room in the house."

"Waal, now. That's kind of ye. It is for a fact. But I hear it said along the trail that your place has bedbugs so it's not fitten for a man of my fame which is more extensible that you may imagine." He drew the letter from his pocket. "I reckon this gentleman is here, and I'd like to make delivery."

The fat man read the envelope. He was undecided and more nervous than ever. His eyes kept traveling from John, to the Navy, to the stairs, and back again. He swallowed and said: "You'll have to leave it. I'll put it in his box. He ain't here."

"I'm a man of religious leanings, and I don't cotton to any breakage of the liar's commandment, being in number the ninth. He's here, and I reckon you'll direct me to him."

The fat man shook his head and whispered: "No." Sweat beaded his forehead. He licked his lips. "No, they'd kill you if you tried to go up there. And they'd kill me, too."

"Would he kill a good friend o' the Confed'racy?" He looked around to make sure that no one was in earshot and, leaning across the counter, spoke the word: "Magnolia."

There was an instantaneous change in the fat man's manner. He took a deep breath and wiped the sweat away. "Where from?"

"Virginny City . . . number six."

"Hail Jeff Davis!"

"And Robbie Lee!"

Following directions given him by the fat man, he climbed some stairs and rapped at a door bearing the numeral 6.

A peephole opened, and an eye studied him.

"Magnolia," he said again. "Virginny City."

There was some muttered conversation in the background, and a voice said: "Name of your commanding officer."

"Officer number fifty-two, Confed'rate Army o' the Nor'-west."

A bolt then grated, the door opened, and he went inside. It was a large room with a row of fancy pillars down the middle. Eighteen or twenty men were seated here and there, but two-thirds of the chairs were empty. Some of the men, on his entrance, had masked themselves with kerchiefs.

He said: "Ye don't need to be suspicious o' me. Why, I was shootin' Abolitonists in Kansas in 'Fifty-Four. Fought all the way through the election. Voted six ballots all in the same day, and every one of 'em for the Southern cause, and I say that's a tol'able record for a man that can't read and write beyond the letter X."

A tall masked man at the front of the room said: "Hello, John."

John said—"Waal, now!"—and hitched up his heavy gun belts.

The man came around the table where he had been seated, apparently conducting the meeting. He was slim, but his movements gave evidence of power. He wore a coat and trousers of British parsley mix, riding shoes, and a white linen shirt. Around his waist, rather high, was strapped a dressed-up Navy with ivory stocks.

John said: "I heered that voice before, but from 'way yonder, and a long time ago. Be ye from Californy?"

The man unfastened the handkerchief, revealing his face. It was an extremely long face with a small mouth and a nose that overhung at the tip, forming what was commonly referred to as a pickle nose. He was in his middle or late thirties.

John's eyes grew narrow, and there was a hardening of the muscles at the sides of his jaw as he masticated the tobacco. "Why, damn," he said, "it's Spade Crews!"

He had learned at the mission that the letter was addressed to someone named Crews, but he hadn't associated it with this man he had known along the Oregon Trail. In those days Crews had worn a beard cut to a point after the manner of a doctor. It had been the beard that won him the name Spade, and not, as was popularly supposed, his record for burying those hapless emigrants whom he robbed with the connivance of renegade Indians while operating Fort Grande Ronde between Boise and the Umatilla. Later, with the surge of gold seekers to the bonanzas of Snake River and Montana, Crews was reputed to have made a fortune trading stolen horses, and, further, to have grown respectable and been elected to the Oregon Legislature.

Comanche John shook hands with him. He rubbed his palm downward across his homespuns to take away the unclean feeling, and said: "Waal, Spade, I haven't seen you since that night at Sody Crick when. . . ."

"We won't go *digging* into the past, will we?" Crews asked, making his joke on the word *spade*. He went on with a sharp-toothed smile: "Start digging into past records in *this* camp and everyone would be embarrassed!"

John's hand, in his pocket, felt the letter. The letter would mean the end of a damn'-Yankee spy by the name of Mark Clay, but for all that he decided to wait for a while. There had been a rumor around that this Last Chance chapter of the Confederate organization had been operating with an eye to its own profit rather than the profit of the Southern cause. Up until now he had discounted such reports, but with Spade Crews here. . . .

Crews asked: "Well, how are things with our brothers in Virginia City?"

"Tolerable. If everybody was ready as the loyal sons o' the South in Virginny City, you wouldn't have to hold this meeting behind a peephole door. This Territory would already be lined up to the Confed'racy."

A short, well-dressed man with mutton-chop whiskers got to his feet and said sharply: "I, seh, resent the imputations inhcrent in that remark. The Last Chance chapter would long ago have joined or exceeded any otheh group in readiness if the arms and munitions duly paid for by us had been delivered as per agreement, and not hawged, yes, I say *hawged,* by you swaggering swashbucklers at Alder Gulch."

"Them guns was sent, cap'n. I was to the meeting, myself, three weeks ago, when the matter was brought up. And not only were they sent, but they were delivered and signed for. Better'n a hundred rifles, twenty-five of 'em Spencers captured off that Army supply train at Fort Laramie."

The man cried: "No such guns were delivered! And I'll wager they weren't sent." He looked at Crews. "What is your judgment on this, Colonel?"

Crews laughed and shrugged. The corners of his small mouth were twisted down. He looked down the end of his pickle nose. "My judgment is that our visitor from Virginia City has been misinformed."

The little man assumed a senatorial pose with one hand on his heart. "I've heard such accusations befoah, emanating from the inhabitants of those camps to the south who call themselves Southern patriots, and I don't mind saying, seh, that I have grown resentful. Someone is getting away with these arms, seh . . . getting away with them for their own profit . . . the arms for which we have paid. And I for one demand an investigation."

"Sure, Appleby," Crews said. "But it will have to be taken up before the full assembly."

"Then I *intend* to take it up before the assembly." Appleby turned his attention back to Comanche John. His face was florid. He mopped it off. "Who are *you* to come around heah impugning the loyalty of the Last Chance organization?"

"Whoa up, now, whoa up! Let's not get to fightin' amongst ourselves like a bunch of Yankees. I didn't come here to touch any sore spots or stir up any old argyments."

He moved back, hooked a chair with a toe of his jackboot, sat in it the wrong way with his hands folded across the back, a position that was perfectly careless but just by chance left both Navies free. He chewed, and let his eyes rove, wondering which one of the men here was the Union spy, Mark Clay.

There was a period of silence. One of the men looked at his watch. They were waiting for something. Crews paced the room, stopped at the window, pulled a shade aside, and looked down on the gulch street below.

"See anything?" somebody asked.

"Seem to be getting a posse together down at the express office."

"Who . . . Bower?"

"No. Carmichael."

Comanche John knew that Carmichael was the deputy U.S. marshal.

Appleby laughed and looked at his watch. "An hour and a half after the stage was robbed they go looking for the bandits, and that at Birdtail Pass!"

Crews turned from the window and said: "That mail sack wasn't lost at Birdtail. It was lost after the coach arrived in Last Chance."

Appleby muttered: "Hare-brained idea, using the mails for our dispatches instead of a special courier."

One of the others said: "How would you like to ride horseback with letters between here and Salt Lake City, Appleby?"

Appleby ignored the question. He paced the room and stopped to address Crews: "Do you think there's any necessity of keeping the men here any longer? That mail will never be recovered."

Crews spun from the window. "I tell you, they'll stay where they are!"

The look-out moved his shotgun a trifle, showing he was ready to enforce any command that Crews made.

"This is madness!" Appleby exclaimed.

It was the first inkling Comanche John had that at least some of the men were being held against their wills. He wondered which was Mark Clay. He drawled—"Mark, you know something of guns."—and saw a young, good-looking, dark-haired man jerk erect with surprise at hearing his name called. Comanche John drawled on: "Now, what in your opinion is the advantage of the Spencer rifle over the old-time Jager?"

Mark Clay started to answer and changed his mind: "I never fired a Spencer in my life."

Crews was looking at them. "I didn't know you two were acquainted."

Comanche John said: "I git around by day and by night." He stood up very casually, scratched, and pulled up his gun belts. "Waal, now that I've paid my visit, I think I'll be leaving ye."

"You'll stay where you are!"

The look-out, with his shotgun still crosswise on his knees, leaned forward. Crews stood straight, his arm dangling below his fancy Navy Colt.

A rangy man with a reddish mustache was up, his thumbs hooked in crossed belts weighed by two Navies. They had him on three sides. John regarded them with the appreciation of a connoisseur. "Now thar's a scene that fills my heart with bee-attytude. That's a twenty-four karat word I picked up from a preacher. It means I'm glad at the power us Rebs can toss at the Yankees whenever it seems more important to fight them than to fight amongst ourselves. And maybe line our own pockets in the meantime. Whoa, whoa now! Not accusing anybody. Not saying that any man in *this* room sold a Spencer rifle to a Blackfoot chief."

Crews was rigid. He opened and closed his right hand. He said through his teeth: "Sit down!"

John made no move to comply. The letter in his pocket made him uncomfortable. He should never have mentioned it to the fat man. His safety demanded that he either deliver it or make his getaway. He chewed, sent a stream of tobacco juice across the floor, and went on in his drawling voice: "Now, the way I look at the situation is this. Thar's three of ye. I could kill you, Crews, with my right-hand Navy, and the look-out yonder with my left, but I'd have the red-headed gent left over. So, I'd like to settle this in a parley-mentary way, appealing to your reason." He spat, and hitched up his pants. "As ye know, I'm a stranger here, having just arrove. How did I come? . . . ye may ask. Not horseback, and not afoot, but by conveyance . . . to wit, a stagecoach. A stage-coach over Birdtail Pass. Yep, I was on 'er. I seen the robber. What's more, I been in pretty close touch with the man that heisted the mail sack. Now, if ye'd like that mail sack more'n ye would my company, you release me and I'll be more gratyfied to fetch it to ye."

Crews asked: "Was it *you* who robbed that coach?"

"*Me* rob a coach? Why, I'm innocent as a babe unborn. I wouldn't think of robbing a stagecoach, and especially one headed inside without any gold on her. No, gents, it'll do no good holding me here. You give it your thought, which you want most, the pleasure of my company or that missing mail sack."

One of the men, who all the while had been masked, tore the kerchief off, wiped sweat from his face, and said: "Let him go. What harm can it do? I'm tired of sitting here, being held prisoner in this high-handed manner. I'll have you know, Colonel Crews, that I'm as important in this organization as you, and. . . ."

"But you're forgetting this is a *military* organization, and I am the commanding officer. I'll give you the facts straight out. One of us is a spy. Yes, maybe one right here in this room. Three days ago I received a communication from officer member number eight-one in Salt Lake City that the Confederate organization of the West is riddled with informers, and that one of them, a regular Army officer, had been assigned to us, here in Last Chance. Officer eight-one promised that he would have the name of that spy in the next mail north, and that mail was robbed tonight. Obviously I couldn't bring it up at our meeting without informing the spy himself. Only three men knew of it, commissioned officers of this organization . . . myself, Major Appleby, and Major Stillman who at this moment is out learning the facts of the mail theft. I have kept you here for one obvious reason. If one of you, one of us, is the spy. . . ."

"*He* couldn't be a spy," the man said, indicating John. "Why, he's never attended one of our meetings."

"He could warn the spy if he isn't in this room."

"I hate to make this ree-mark, Colonel," John said, "but your bucket has a hole in it. You're keeping the letter a secret, but the spy must know about it or why'd he lift it off the coach?" He let it sink in. "O' course, I can't guarantee to get the mail sack if ye keep me here too long."

Others commenced to raise their voices. They were tired of waiting. Many had gone without supper.

Indecision showed in Crews's manner, so, seizing the moment, John slouched to the door and said to the look-out: "Open it up."

Crews said nothing to stop him, so the look-out obeyed, and a moment later Comanche John was outside in the hall.

IV

He blew out his breath, muttered against the unseasonable warmth, took off his black slouch hat, and wiped sweat from his forehead. He reached the top of the stairs just in time to see the fat clerk hurry outside. "Stillman!" the clerk called.

That would be Major Stillman whom Crews had mentioned. He felt in his pocket to make certain the letter was still there, walked down, through the lobby, and outside. The clerk, talking to a heavy-booted, square-jawed man on the sidewalk below, did not see him.

Loafers still occupied the green benches around the porch. None of them paid more than casual attention as John walked around on the dining room side, left the porch by some side stairs, and followed a footpath hacked from the rocky rise of the gulch.

Down on the street four horsemen went past at a good clip, weaving in and out among the stagnated freight outfits. A light now burned in the parson's mission, and over the *clump* of boots and the cursing and bawling of teamsters he could hear the *whine* of the organ and a nasal voice singing aggressively:

Revive me in the waters of Gal-il-ee!
Restore me with the blood of the Lamb!

A thick knot of men stood outside, looking in, and the parson, striding among the empty benches, was trying to urge them inside. "Come inside and bask in the glory of everlasting light. Climb up from the black gulch o' sin!"

John watched for a while, chewed, and cursed his luck. He took the letter from his pocket, tempted to tear it up, decided against it, and started on a course that would take him around to the rear of the mission.

He walked in the shadow along a Chinese washee. He stopped on the sidewalk. All seemed peaceful. He started across.

From the shadow at his back he heard the metallic *click* of a gun hammer being drawn to cock. His hands started by reflex toward the butts of his Navies, but he checked himself. He stood rigidly. His eyes, rolled to look at an angle behind him, were fastened on the blue shine of gunmetal.

"One move and I'll kill you," a man said.

John let out a long breath. "That'd be a waste o' bullets, because ye got me without." He spread his fingers and kept his hands wide. "I'm just a peaceful, wayfarin' pilgrim off the dark trails o' the night called to repentance by the sound o' that music yonder, and ye wouldn't want to harm a man just enterin' upon the threshold of a new life."

He turned slowly. A big, raw-boned miner with a face lop-sided from tobacco held two Navies on him. He was not alone. Men came up on both sides of him.

One of them said: "You're entering on a new life, all right." He laughed. "Git that, boys? I said he was entering on a new life. Meant he was going to git hung, see?"

Nobody else laughed. The miner said to John: "All right, take off that ornery old hat so we can have a look at your face. How about it, Rupe? Is this him?"

"It's him!" the third man said with a note of awe in his voice. "Damned if we haven't captured Comanche John."

John hee-hawed and beat dust from his pants. "Who, *me?* Ye think I'm Comanche John? Now, boys, you got your tails out of the crupper. You'd be the laughing stock o' the country if ye was to hang me for that unreligious Comanche John. Why, I'm associated with the parson, yonder. Practically a man o' the cloth."

"Keep your hands clear." Standing behind him, the miner lifted his Navies. "Sky pilot, hey? Seems to me this is considerable steel for a sky pilot to be totin' around."

"Not in a sinful camp like Last Chance it ain't."

With a gun rammed in his spine, John was marched up the walk. It seemed strange to be without the weight of his Navies. Already word of his capture had raced along the street, and men came hurrying from both directions.

"They got him!" a boy kept shouting. "They took Comanche John!"

John asked over his shoulder: "Suppose, just for argyment, I *was* Comanche John . . . what sort of a charge do ye have trumped up ag'in' me?"

"Highway robbery."

He whistled. "Ye mean that Birdtail business?"

"Name your robbery, you've pulled enough of 'em."

A short, officious man in a dusty black suit and knee-high riding boots pushed through, using a gun and a quirt to nudge men aside, and said: "Find anything on him?"

"We don't need to find anything on *this* one." The miner hitched his pants and swaggered a little. "This is the big one. This one we can hang on general principles. This one is Comanche John!"

John asked: "You the U.S. marshal?"

"I'm Carmichael, deputy U.S. marshal."

"Then ye must be level-headed enough to know ye can't hang a man that's already been hung in Boise City. And in Yaller Jacket, too, for that matter. See that mission, yonder?

The parson will tell ye who I. . . ."

"The parson is the one who sent us after you."

"No-o!" John took a deep breath. He suddenly looked beat out and tired. He rubbed his head with his old slouch hat and left it halfway over his eyes. "The parson told ye! He turnt against me. He said he would, and, by grab, he did."

"Where's that letter you took from the bag?"

"Letter?" John was crafty again. He chewed and spat. Down the street he could hear the parson's magpie voice shouting for people to make way. "That letter I deelivered to its proper destination."

"Search him!"

John tried to pull away, but the miner had him on one side and Rupe on the other. The third man went through his pockets, turning up some pistol charges, a Barlow knife, and the letter.

John said: "I confess all. I took that letter from the parson. Give it back to him."

Carmichael, holding the envelope high to read it by the light of a window above the crowd, said: "This doesn't belong to the parson. It's addressed to Crews at the London Hotel."

The parson was fighting forward. "Give me that letter!"

"What right you got to the letter?"

The parson cried: "That's addressed to Crews! We all know what Crews is . . . him and his Rebels, meeting every day at that hotel, swaggering around, pushing honest folk off the walks, talking about what'll happen when the Confederacy takes the country over. That letter is Confederate business. . . ."

"Keep him off me!" Carmichael shouted to his men. He thrust the letter inside his coat, beyond the parson's reach. "This is part of the United States Mail, and it will be delivered as such."

As Comanche John, surrounded by guards, was taken down the sidewalk toward jail, the parson stayed with him. "Ye didn't give it to him, John! Ye didn't deliver it, after all. John, I'm proud. I'm proud, and I'm ashamed I set 'em after ye. Behold, I may be the cause of getting ye hung, but I brought ye to the mourner's bench of repentance, and I say, which is the more important, a man's soul or the bones in his neck? John, don't ye worry about a thing, it's my bounden promise, I'll see to it ye git the finest funeral ever preached in this sinful camp of Last Chance."

The crowd was left behind at the front door of the jail.

Carmichael, the first man in, said: "Prisoner for you, Bower, and keep him under guard."

Bower was the big, heavy-footed man John had seen earlier in the night. He gulped and said: "Why, damn it if it ain't the holy pilgrim back to try out the jail!"

"I out-fooled myself, all right," John said. "I thought I was mighty wise, but you fellows here in Last Chance was just one frame wiser. No use denying it. Ye got me nailed for sure. The cyards of life are all dealt from the deck, and hyar I am without even openers. I'm a man o' simple tastes. All I ask is a fair trial, a stout rope, and a good drop. Time for prayer and time to write to my loved ones back in Pike County, Missouri."

"Lock him up," Carmichael said. "They had him in jail in Lewiston, and he gave them the slip. I don't want any slips here."

"Maybe you think *you* ought to run this jail!" Bower said.

"I don't want any more trouble with you. You know the agreement. . . ."

"Don't jangle over me, boys," John said. "This is a tender moment in my life, being nigh onto my last, and it grieves me sore to think I'd stirred up discord betwixt you gent'men of the law. Now, if ye will delay a minute, I'd like to make full confession. Yep, I'm guilty. Robbed the coach. Me beside the driver and my pardner on the ground. We robbed the mails, and not a pennyweight of advantage did we git from it, so let that be a lesson to you young lads when you're tempted to ride down that long, one-way coulée beyond the law."

Carmichael asked: "Who was your partner?"

"Now, I'll tell you that, too. Young lad by the handle of Mark Clay, and right now he's sitting in a second-story room in the London Hotel."

The parson, crowding through the door said: "John, be ye crazy?"

He answered from the side of his mouth, "Loco as a four-dollar pony when I get down to saving the hide of a Yankee spy. How long do you suppose he'll stay alive once Spade Crews gits his hands on that letter? Let 'em arrest him."

Bower cried: "Here, what you two talking about?"

"Just getting solace from this ordained minister of the Holy Word. Aye, for I am a stranger amongst ye and sore pressed, and that's straight from the Psalms o' David, it is for a fact." He laid a hand on the parson's shoulder. "Know all men by these presents, this is my final will and testament. All my worldly goods including my two Navy Colts I do hereby bequeath to the Reverend Jeremiah Parker, so hand 'em over to him, you stranglers, because I know my rights under the Territorial law."

Bower, with a gun in one hand and a big brass key in the other, said: "You're not putting the blinders on *me* with that sky-pilot talk. I'm locking you up."

With John inside the cell and the lock turned, Bower puffed out his breath and apparently felt better. He said: "All right, *now* you can deliver your solace and be damned."

He still didn't move. He watched narrowly as the parson

and John talked through the little grated window.

The parson said: "John, I'm going to the Territorial governor and ask for a reprieve."

"Don't waste your time. You take them guns I willed ye. And slip 'em behind that rain bar'l out front."

"Ye won't stand a chance, John. When they take ye out of here, you'll be three deep in deppities and trussed like a Christmas pig. No, we might as well face it. Your luck's run out. John, this time you're going to git hung."

"Don't you worry about me, Parson. It's no joke about me being an old woolly wolf from the Rawhide Mountains. I drifted many a mile, and I lost some toes in the trap, and it's seldom if ever I git run inside a hole that ain't got a blind door some place. You collect them Navies and do with 'em as I say."

V

Comanche John tried out the bunk. It was filled with hay, covered with a ratty old quilt. Deep, toward the wall, was a lump, but the lump did not bother him. He lay full length, hands folded across his chest, his black slouch hat over his eyes. He seemed to sleep.

Men kept coming to the door to look inside. He could hear the clump and drag of boots and the mingled voices of men in the front room and, muffled by thick walls, the crowds along the gold camp street. Slowly the noise diminished. Whole minutes would pass with no word being spoken by those in the front room. He could hear the distant whine of a fiddle playing the "Virginia Minuet." He hummed with the music. The lump deep in the hay was comforting, and he kept his right hip resting on it.

The light was cut off at the grated peephole in the door, and he knew that someone was peering in at him.

"He's a cool one, all right," Bower said. "You suppose he's the real Comanche John, or do you suppose he was just bragging?"

"Hell of a thing to brag about," a voice answered from the front room. "A man wouldn't brag himself into a hang rope."

Bower turned from the door and said: "That damned deppity marshal, hinting I wasn't man enough to hold him in jail! Where is he, anyhow? Still across the street, meeting with his law and order society? I wouldn't think they'd ponder very long what to do with *this* rattlesnake."

The other man asked something, and Bower answered: "Sure, I feel better. I won't rest easy till his neck is pulled out a foot long! Used to be, when I first came to the country four or five years ago, they hung 'em five minutes after they caught 'em. Now Carmichael comes along and they have to get the vigilantes together and vote on it. I guess civilization is all right, and it was bound to come, but I liked 'er better the way she was."

Comanche John sat up, yawned, and groped under him to the lump in the hay. It was made by the gun he had placed there while inspecting the cell earlier that night. It was a Derringer, a cheap, double-barreled piece, smooth bore, loaded with buckshot. He yawned, blew hay out of the barrels, inspected the loads to make sure both percussion caps were in place. Then he walked to the door.

"Be it mornin' yet?" he asked.

Bower came to the grating and suddenly froze with the double Derringer six inches from his forehead.

"Don't say a word," John said softly. "That's it. Live for a while. Raise a family and tame the wild Nor'west. Let somebody else go down in history books as the man that hung

Comanche John. Somebody left this gun layin' around, and I don't look gift horses in the mouth. Waal, I *did* look this one, and counted her teeth, and I'm glad to inform ye that there's an even dozen in each bar'l. Buckshot, that is. Now, open up. Real quiet."

The voice from the front room said: "What's going on?"

John said: "Answer bright, now."

"Not a thing," Bower said shakily.

The key made a grating sound in the lock. The door was free, and John shouldered it enough to get through. He made his move quickly. The Derringer was briefly blocked off by the heavy planks, but Bower made no move for his guns. He retreated with his hands wide of his body. John would have demanded Bower's pistols, but a shadow against the lamp told him the other man was out of his chair, coming to investigate.

The man saw Bower, took alarm, and went for his Colts. John fired at the lamp and smashed it with a charge of buckshot.

He dived forward. The room, suddenly dark, was ripped by gunfire. There were wild bullets and flying splinters, but John had rolled to his feet on the sidewalk out front.

He took a deep breath of the cool night air. He fired the second barrel inside, aiming low. The buckshot roared into the floor and made a hard rattle against an inside wall. He found the rain barrel. His Navies were there, stuck between it and the log wall.

"Good old parson," he muttered.

"It's Comanche John!" Bower was shouting. "Git him out there, somebody!"

Carmichael and his men poured from some meeting rooms across the street. Bullets thudded against the wall, glanced screeching from the hard-beaten street. They punched holes through the rain barrel. Moving swiftly, Comanche John answered with a stream of lead from both Navies.

"Come on, ye Yankee yellabellies, step up and take your turn. Thar's enough for one and all. *Yippee,* I was raised on corn likker and country sorghum. I pick my teeth with the cactus bush and drink water out of the crick like a horse. I got cemeteries named after me all the way from Fraser River to Yuba Gulch, so give me room, because I'm Comanche John, the one they wrote the opry about."

He found cover behind a barrel, beyond a watering trough that soon sprayed water like a sprinkling wagon, and moved on his knees behind a segment of platform walk. Bullets tore splinters and showered him with stinging rock fragments from the street. He retreated like a crab, boots first. Carmichael was shouting commands, trying to get some order in the pursuit.

John climbed a rain barrel hidden by shadow. He chinned himself over the edge of a roof. The building was a Chinese washee, low and flat. He bellied across it, and dropped to the ground out back. He stopped to reload. There were seven charges they'd left in his pockets, patent charges of powder and ball wrapped in oiled paper. He rammed them home, fixed the percussion caps. Gunfire still volleyed in the street. He chuckled, spat, walked across a vacant space through heaps of ashes and bottles to a path that took him up the rocky side of the gulch.

"Quite a party," he said. "Quite . . . a . . . party!"

Comanche John was winded. Sweat made the band of his hat slick so it wanted to slide around on his head. Somewhere he had lost his chew of tobacco. The mission was below him. He dropped downhill to its rear door. Candles burned, but the parson was not there.

He holstered his Navies and walked on to the front sidewalk. A man collided with him, and he asked: "What the thunder's going on?"

"Comanche John!" the man cried. "They got him cornered by the assay office."

"The famous road agent from Californy?"

John walked on. The street now was almost deserted. A young man with a curly brown beard and long, curly hair was seated on the edge of the walk, bent over, holding the fleshy part of his shoulder. His teeth were gritted, and blood oozed between his fingers. He had evidently been hit by a stray bullet.

John took from his mouth the fresh chew of tobacco he had worked up and handed it to him. "Hyar, son, I feel sort of responsible for that, so hold this tobacky to it."

He walked on, watching the second story of the London Hotel. The shades were drawn with reddish strips of light showing around them. A sound made him wheel around with a Navy unholstered.

"Oh, you, gal," he said, seeing who it was. "How's the coach business?"

"Where is he?" she asked. She had been crying, but now she was too distracted to cry.

"Who? Mark Clay? I thought Carmichael would have him in custody by this time." His eyes narrowed. "Say, some busybody didn't go and deliver that letter to Crews up yonder at the hotel!"

"I don't know what happened to the letter. Stillman might have got hold of it. Or my father."

"Your father? What's your name, gal?"

"Lyn Appleby."

"Major Appleby. So that's how ye learned about the letter."

"We'll have to do something."

"Now, I been a mite tied up, or I would have. Whar's the parson?"

"At the hotel. I told him the password, and. . . ."

"And now he's fixing to get kilt."

Running, Comanche John climbed the steps to the London Hotel's big front porch. The benches were all unoccupied save for one where a drunk was sleeping and snoring. He went inside. The lobby was empty. It was gassy and close-smelling. Something smarted his throat. He could hear the *clump* of hurrying boots somewhere above. The gassy smell came to him, more strongly than before. It was the odor of burning wood and spilled lamp oil.

He heard a muffled cry for help—the voice of a man behind a gag—the parson's voice. He started up the stairs two steps at a time. A man loomed suddenly above—the guardsman with his sawed-off shotgun. John spun to one side, left hand on the balustrade, right holding his Navy, and fired. He felt the whip of flying buckshot overhead. The guard was hit and knocked down. He struck on his shoulders and the back of his head, and slid feet first down the stairs. He was unconscious.

John stepped over him.

Crews's voice asked: "Who's there?"

"Me, Comanche John!"

Bullet lead and streaks of flame cut the hall in a sudden cross volley. Walking forward, Comanche John aimed at the flashes. There were seven or eight explosions, all so close that two seconds would have blanketed them all. He kept on through dense smoke and stopped over the prostrate body of Spade Crews. "Headed the wrong way," he muttered. "You was scairt, and you got kilt. You can't fight and run away at the same time. So that pays ye for all them poor pilgrims ye robbed in I-dee-ho."

The door to the big room was locked. He shouldered through it. One end of the room, doused with oil, was all ablaze. The smoke was blinding, but against the red of fire he could see a man on his knees, fighting the bonds that held him hand and foot. The man was young Mark Clay.

John reached in his pocket and remembered that they'd taken his knife from him. He tripped over a second man who lay bound on the floor.

"John!" the parson said, his voice muffled by a cloth gag. "John, ye made it! Ye got out o' that jail!"

"Parson, I got eight-dollar Derringers cached in jails all the way from Sonora to Kootenai House. Ye got a knife?"

He worked with the knots while holding his breath, trying not to breathe fumes. With the parson freed, he got Mark Clay on his feet, then groped through the door, down the hall, and followed the smell of fresh air down some back stairs.

The parson said: "What's all that shooting?"

"Why, they got somebody cornered yonder. Have an idee it's Comanche John, but danged if I'm going yonder to tell 'em their mistake."

Mark Clay, coughing smoke, gasped: "I'll get you . . . government pardon. A promise. I'll name you in my report. You saved the Union cause."

John seized him by the collar. He held him at arm's length and bellowed: "No, ye won't! This is a secret, you hear? I got a dear old mother back in Missouri, and she's proud o' me now. How'd she feel knowing I helped a Union spy? If ye really feel like paying me back, find me a horse and a saddle . . . a fast-traveling horse, if ye don't mind, and one that can go a distance, because this camp shows every sign of becoming inhospitable, and I don't be one to stay where I ain't wanted."

* * * * *

It was almost dawn. Wind, on the mountain ridge, carried the chill feel of snow from the higher Rockies to the north. Comanche John, after long riding, reined in, and pulled his buckskin vest closer around him. Miles away and below, a serpentine string of lights marked the course of Last Chance Gulch, and a glowing rectangle showed the remains of the London Hotel.

"Yankee," he said, "a real, likely lad, too. Now how'd a man like that pick up with the wrong side? Probably born so far north he couldn't help himself." His body was slack and slouched in the saddle, his shapeless black hat rested on the back of his head, and then his voice lifted in song:

Comanche John is a highwayman
He hails from County Pike,
And whenever he draws his Navies out
'Tis share and share alike. . . .

About the Author

Dan Cushman was born in Osceola, Michigan, and grew up on the Cree Indian Reservation in Montana. He graduated from the University of Montana with a Bachelor of Science degree in 1934 and pursued a career in mining as a prospector, assayer, and geologist before turning to journalism. In the early 1940s his novelette-length stories began appearing regularly in such Fiction House magazines as *North-West Romances* and *Frontier Stories*. Later in the decade his North-Western and Western stories as well as fiction set in the Far East and Africa began appearing in *Action Stories*, *Adventure*, and *Short Stories*. *Stay Away, Joe*, which first appeared in 1953, is an amusing novel about the mixture, and occasional collision, of Indian culture and Anglo-American culture among the Métis (French Indians) living on a reservation in Montana. The novel became a bestseller and remains a classic to this day, greatly loved especially by Indian peoples for its truthfulness and humor. Yet, while humor became Cushman's hallmark in such later novels as *The Old Copper Collar* (1957) and *Good Bye, Old Dry* (1959), he also produced significant historical fiction in *The Silver Mountain* (1957), concerned with the mining and politics of silver in Montana in the 1890s. This novel won a Spur Award from the Western Writers of America. His fiction remains notable for its breadth, ranging all the way from a story of the cattle frontier in *Tall Wyoming* (1957) to a poignant and memorable portrait of small-town life in Michigan just before the Great War in *The Grand and the Glorious* (1963). *The Return of Comanche John* will be his next Five Star Western.